LOVE-IN-A-MIST

By the same author:

Casting a Shadow, The Book Guild, 1997

LOVE-IN-A-MIST

Arthur Wilson

The Book Guild Ltd
Sussex, England

This book is a work of fiction. The characters and situations in this story are imaginary. No resemblance is intended between these characters and any real persons, either living or dead.

The Book Guild Ltd
25 High Street,
Lewes, Sussex

First published 1998

Set in Meridien

Typesetting by Wordset
Hassocks, West Sussex

Printed in Great Britain by
Bookcraft (Bath) Ltd, Avon

A catalogue record for this book is
available from the British Library

ISBN 1 85776 242 8

When comforts are declining,
He grants the soul again
A season of clear shining
To cheer it after rain.

William Cowper
1731 – 1800

1

Less than a mile going north of Porchester was a small, close-knit group of modern-built houses. This group in no way constituted a village with its inhabitants of ruddy complexions and a squire with horses, as one might expect. There was not even a village shop. The houses were built on land a little higher than the road which passed by. In the front garden of one of these houses was an eye-catching display of roses, for it was then late June. In the house lived just a very ordinary family, not particularly rich but certainly not poor. The lady of the house was Claire Rowena Halliday, one of style, with chestnut hair, large blue eyes and, overall, a face with softness; a woman 30 years of age and always well-dressed. Before the birth of her only child she had been a receptionist in a local hotel. Claire had enjoyed this type of work, mainly because she was not basically a career girl but a friendly one who loved meeting people. In fact, it was in the hotel that she first met her prospective husband.

Our acquaintance with this family begins early on a Sunday morning with Claire in the front garden picking a few roses for the breakfast table. Roses were Claire's favourite flowers and irrespective of the fact that throughout winter the bushes and standards were no more than bunches of seemingly dry sticks, she still loved them and, as the gardener of the family, constantly tended a row of standard roses on each side of the pathway leading up to the front door of the house. Her friends and even the postman had constantly complimented her on the display. Each rose was carefully labelled and its likes and dislikes of fertilizer, together with its capacity for fighting off the ravages of disease and insects, were well-imprinted in Claire's mind. She went back into the house and put the roses into a vase which she placed on the table at one end of the combined kitchen and dinette, then continued laying the table for breakfast. Soon her husband, Lionel, appeared, not fully dressed and ready to go as Claire was, but in a dressing gown and, in fact, looking rather untidy.

'Morning, darling' (his usual greeting – Claire much preferred this to 'Hello, old girl' which he claimed was a term of endearment, not an indication of age), 'didn't know you'd left me.'

'Oh, you were so fast asleep, I hadn't the heart to wake you,' she replied. 'Ready for breakfast?'

He nodded assent and sat down. Lionel was clearly made of sterner stuff. He had dark hair which was already beginning to recede and was cut moderately. His eyes were brown with bushy eyebrows. He was always clean-shaven and when breakfast was over, would soon be well-dressed: in fact every inch an executive. He gave the appearance of a man not to be trifled with, was well-known in the local town and was the head of a small private company dealing in general financial and insurance matters. Lionel was well-qualified academically and devoted to his profession, sometimes, it seemed, to the exclusion of everything else. With an insatiable appetite for work, he could only be applauded for the company ran well and was expanding, thus financially Claire and their son were well-provided for. In view of Lionel's workload he found it more difficult in coming to terms with country living and being involved in local events than did Claire.

'Seen anything of Philip yet?' he continued.

'Not yet,' she replied. 'He's probably still in bed. Shall I give him a call?'

'No, leave him up there. It'd be nice to have breakfast on our own for once,' Lionel replied. 'Let sleeping dogs lie.'

They sat down to enjoy their breakfast in peace but not for long. In came the apple of their eyes, a young, bright little lad some seven years of age. He was truly his parents' pride and joy even though they had to admit to each other (but seldom to anybody else) that he could be a handful and was not always easy to manage. He was classed by his father sometimes as a 'cheeky little devil'.

'Hullo, Mum, hullo, Dad,' the boy announced, 'what's for breakfast? I'm hungry.' Which was nothing new, he was always hungry.

Claire had one rather special skill, that of a well-above average pianist and Lionel had done his best to see that she had a piano worthy of her. Hence, in earlier days, they had exchanged their rather old upright instrument for a grand, not a full grand for that would have over-filled their drawing room, but a small one, a grand nevertheless. It was, in fact, part of Claire, the two were inseparable. When Claire was no more than six years old, her mother had decided to become a pianist. As with so many people, it all looked so simple, just practise each day and, hey presto!, success and perhaps even fame are soon within one's grasp. However, it was not to be. The music teacher came once a week to try to bridge the formidable gap between Claire's mother and the intended musical scales. It was therefore inevitable that the would-be pianist soon found that it was not so easy and the desire to play gradually left her. While discussing the fact that her progress seemed to be abnormally slow and that both she and also her teacher were becoming frustrated and more than a little disappointed with the whole idea, Claire was heard tinkling on the keyboard.

'What about the little girl instead, then?' suggested the music teacher.

'Oh, she's too young,' answered Claire's mother, 'she's only six.'

'That's not too young,' came the reply. 'It's an ideal age to start – and look, she's keen to play already.'

So Claire had her piano lessons regularly and loved it all, even though it was terribly hard work. She soon passed the stage of 'In a Monastery Garden' when most budding pianists give up and went on to Beethoven, Chopin and Rachmaninov, her favourite composers, some ten years' hard work, but in fact ten years of happiness. During this time and since, she was welcomed and very popular at local concerts and parties where a piano was available.

A few houses away lived Claire's close friend, Pearl Cartwright. She and Claire had been through school as close chums and their friendship was still unshaken.

Pearl was a reasonably attractive girl, not as tall as Claire and with shorter wavy hair which seemed to change colour every few months. She had never married, mainly because, although previously a working girl, she thought she was needed by her parents for her father, though only in his late fifties, suffered from angina. There was no doubt, however, that Pearl was concerned about her future security and would have liked to get married, especially considering that her friend Claire had done so long ago. However, Pearl was, in fact, seeing a well-off man, Henry Reardon-Smythe, who seemed to care for her but never mentioned marriage. That was Pearl's problem.

On the other hand, everything in Claire's garden, both outside and inside, was lovely and life for Claire stayed that way for just over the next two years. However, Lionel was not so fortunate. He had several problems at his work. For a time there seemed to be a continual run of staff difficulties. To begin with, a young lad, moderately intelligent and with promise, whom Lionel was hoping to train so that ultimately he would become a useful member of staff, began arriving late for work and was also difficult to handle by the more senior members of the office. Lionel invoked the usual management techniques in handling the lad but to little avail. There would be some improvement for a few days, then back to square one again. As far as Lionel or any of his staff could find out, the lad had got himself mixed up with a gang of unruly boys and girls and was unwilling to break away for fear of being subjected to ridicule. Eventually Lionel could do no more than give him a written warning containing the threat of dismissal should there be no improvement in his attitude to work. This did not have the desired effect so, reluctantly, after several more warnings, Lionel resigned himself to the inevitable and the boy's employment was terminated.

This was the first occasion on which Lionel had needed to take such action and although he knew he had no option and had done the right thing, for a few days he was a slightly saddened man. Claire was a great help. Usually when they were first tucked up in bed at night, he would tell her of his troubles, she would listen sympathetically and make him feel that each step he had taken was the right one.

Soon after this problem, the young lady who did most of the word-processing also seemed to be full of troubles. She had a slight accident with her car. It was the other driver's fault but happily little damage was done and her car was soon on the road again. However, that did not seem to be the end of the matter for she began to be absent from work and, peculiarly enough, often reported sick on a Monday. Lionel was beginning to find that instead of handling financial arrangements, he seemed to be beset with staff problems. He called the young lady into his office for a chat.

'Miss Sheridan, or perhaps I may call you Veronica, I've asked you to see me because your sick leave seems to be getting out of hand.'

'Well, Mr Halliday, I can't help that,' she replied.

'What does the doctor say about you?' he asked.

'Oh, I haven't seen a doctor. There's no need if it's only a day now and again, or is there?'

'Well no,' he replied, 'but your work gets behind and that holds up other people. What can be done to get you fit again?'

'Oh, I'm feeling better than I did so I should be OK. I'm sorry if my absences have upset the office but, honestly, I haven't felt well at all.'

'All right,' said Lionel. 'I too am sorry in having to talk to you like this. Are you sure you don't need a doctor?'

'No, I'm quite sure, I'll be all right now.' And so the interview ended.

For the next few weeks all went well and with a full staff

Lionel felt that at last he could settle down with all staff problems resolved. It was not to be, however, for Veronica phoned in sick again on a Monday. Lionel let this pass, assuming that it was an isolated incident. He was wrong for it happened again two weeks later. 'That's it,' he thought, 'I must do something about this girl.' Into his office she came, looking rather sheepish.

'Did you see a doctor about your Monday morning problems?' he asked.

'No, Mr Halliday. I don't need a doctor, really.'

'Well, what is it then?' he asked. 'There's something odd because you always go sick on a Monday.'

The girl broke down in tears. Lionel felt embarrassed.

'Have I said something, Veronica?' he asked.

'Oh no, Mr Halliday,' she said through her sobs. 'I knew it would come to this.'

'Whatever is wrong?' Lionel continued. He felt that at last he was getting somewhere. 'Are you telling me that you haven't been ill at all?'

'Yes,' she answered quietly with tears beginning to flow. He handed her a handkerchief.

'Well, come on, Veronica. What is the matter?' he queried.

'Oh, Mr Halliday. I'm in such a mess . . .'

'You certainly seem to be. Now tell me all about it. I won't bite you.'

'Well,' she began slowly. 'You remember my car accident?' He nodded. 'The other driver was such a nice chap and he asked me to go out with him.'

'Well, that's good.' said Lionel. 'Surely that's not all?'

'No,' she replied. 'He's a commercial traveller and when he's in this district we go out together and I stay over the weekend with him in a hotel – that's why it's too late for me to get to work on the Monday mornings, so to avoid embarrassment I've made the excuse of not feeling well.'

'But you could have left him on the Sunday evenings, could you not?'

'I've always wanted to but we love each other and he's always pleaded for me to stay on,' was her answer.

'That's no excuse,' said Lionel. 'Surely your job comes first. I do pay you, you know. You've been thoroughly dishonest with me, Veronica. I ought to terminate your employment right now.'

She burst into a flood of tears again.

'Please don't, Mr Halliday, please. I promise you I won't do it again.'

'You're a good worker, Veronica,' he smiled, 'when you're here. So I'll give you one more chance, one more only. Now you'd better tidy up before you go back into the office. Are you going to marry this chap?'

'I hope so,' she said. 'We get on so well together.'

'Perhaps I'll meet him some day,' called Lionel as the girl went through the door of his office. She smiled back at him, not realizing that he did not really mean what he had just said.

Veronica seemed to settle down and from then on her attendance was perfect. Lionel was glad that the problem had been solved and that he still had a competent word-processing operator. However, his peace of mind was to be shattered again for Veronica burst into his office only a few Mondays later.

'Oh, Mr Halliday,' she said. 'I just had to tell you.' (Oh God, he thought, now I suppose she's pregnant.) 'I've just found out – my new boyfriend, you know, the one I've told you about – is married, actually married. And he's got two kids. I'm not going to see *him* any more.'

'Well, well,' replied Lionel, 'at least you'll be able to settle down now.' ('And so will I,' he thought.)

And he did. Thereafter, life for him became more straightforward and so he was able to concentrate on running and building up his office.

After this, with no major problems at work for Lionel, the Halliday household could then be described as a normal happy family abounding in love and with great expectations.

2

Two years of bliss slipped by. Lionel was expanding the business and prospering. Philip was apparently doing well at school, especially when judged by the amount of homework which kept him so occupied that he had little time left over for watching television. Claire's life seemed to be in apple-pie order, with plenty of friends and, in fact, all that a young mum could want. Her days were fully occupied with running both the home and the rather extensive garden but always with a little time left over for her music. But little did she know that the sword of Damocles was hovering over her.

There was a pathway running alongside the main road which had rather steep steps leading up from it to the front door of the house, definitely not the sort on which to slip up. Each house had its own garage built into the bank on which the house stood. Accordingly, one put the car away and then climbed the steps to the house. Loaded with shopping ready for Philip's ninth birthday, Claire unfortunately slipped at the top of the steps and and fell heavily. It was a bumpy slide to the bottom and by the time she reached the pavement below she was not only dishevelled and with stockings torn beyond belief but also in great pain in her legs and feet. She started to pick herself up but found it impossible. Fortunately for her, a couple in a passing car saw her plight, stopped and came running back to help.

'I can't help a lot because I know so little about first aid but can I help you into your house – this is yours, I presume,' the man said.

Claire nodded. She could hardly speak and the pain seemed to be getting worse. 'Let me carry you as best I can,' the man continued.

'He can manage you all right,' the lady added, 'he's often picked me up in fun and you don't look as heavy as I am.'

Claire nodded again and then managed to speak.

'This is my house, my key is in my handbag over there. I would be grateful . . .'

The lady retrieved the handbag, opened it and took out a key.

'This it?' she asked.

'Yes,' said Claire, 'I am so grateful – thank you for your help.'

A few other onlookers had arrived. The man dismissed them with a wave of his hand.

'No problem,' he said. 'Everything is in hand.' The small crowd gradually dispersed.

He carefully picked Claire up bodily and with the guidance of the lady slowly moved up the steps and carried Claire to her front door. The lady opened the door and they went in. He gently lowered Claire onto a settee.

'Still in pain?' he asked.

'Oh God, yes,' she said, 'it's terrible. Both my ankles hurt but the right one is much worse.'

'Who shall we call?' asked her saviour.

'Oh my husband, please. His phone number is in the book by the telephone. The name is Halliday.'

'You're in a bad state. Surely I ought to call for an ambulance first,' he suggested.

'Perhaps you're right,' she agreed. She gave him her address and he dialled the emergency number for an ambulance. He then managed to telephone Lionel who set off for home immediately, arriving only minutes before the ambulance. The medic in charge of the ambulance team gave Claire a brief examination and decided straightaway that she was a case for the hospital. Little could be done on the spot. They therefore took Claire away on a stretcher, negotiating the hostile steps down to the roadway with great care.

Lionel followed the ambulance in his own car and accompanied her as she was wheeled into the hospital. A cursory examination by a doctor soon assessed the extent of Claire's injuries. Apparently her right ankle was broken and, peculiarly enough, the left ankle was also injured but resulting in no more than a rather nasty sprain. He pronounced the rest of Claire to be in good order. Nevertheless, she would be unable to stand on her own feet for some little while. How long it would be he declined to estimate until X-ray films were available. So Claire, who woke up to a day of promise, was now miles away from home, imprisoned in hospital and very soon to have her lower limbs encased in plaster. It had not been a happy day so far for her but what was even worse, she would not be at home for her only son's birthday.

A few days went by in hospital and to her surprise it was announced that she could go home, but in a wheelchair. Those feet were not to touch the ground until sufficient healing had taken place. A nurse would call each day to minister to her needs. This was better news indeed, especially also to Lionel who together with Philip felt that where they lived was no longer a home without their one and only Claire. Hence, at the appointed time, Claire was duly welcomed home with great joy all round. But life was not going to be so easy for when feet and ankles are out of action, movement around the house in a wheelchair or on crutches becomes very difficult. Moreover, the help provided by the visiting nurse seemed grossly inadequate. Lionel immediately came up with his own solution. He would engage a full-time nurse who could look after all of them – never mind the expense, he could easily afford it.

This he did through a nursing association and the next morning on the doorstep was Miss Ruby Featherstone, complete with her small case of medical equipment.

'Good morning,' she said when Lionel opened the door. 'Here I am to look after Mrs Halliday. I presume you are her husband.'

'There's no denying that,' replied Lionel. 'I'm jolly glad you're here. Please come in.'

Looks a little unconventional for a nurse, he thought –

didn't expect to get one so young and attractive. She certainly had everything in the right places, enhanced by a most alluring smile. Lionel was very relieved and hoped Claire would like her – which she certainly did.

Ruby was efficient and forceful. She bustled around and seemed to take everything in her stride. In fact, she more or less took over the whole household. Claire was relieved and grateful to Lionel for arranging for Ruby's help. As soon as Ruby arrived, Lionel had enquired as to how he paid for her services.

'Oh, direct to the association,' she had replied. "They take their whack and I only get what's left.'

Ruby apparently lived on her own in a flat on the other side of the town. She naturally had her own car so did not leave the Hallidays until quite late each evening after she had put Claire to bed. In fact, they all became good friends. After a few days, however, her little car gave up the ghost temporarily and she arrived a little later in the morning having travelled by bus with one change on the way. By evening both Claire and Lionel were uneasy about her travelling back to her flat by public transport on her own. Accordingly, Lionel offered to drive her back home and this he did. Ruby was very grateful because waiting for buses in the late evening was certainly not to be recommended, especially for young ladies.

Thus a few more days went well, with Claire getting better rapidly. With Ruby's help she even got back to her beloved piano, although use of the pedals was rather restricted. But it was not long before doubts began to creep in for it seemed that Ruby's car was having abnormal difficulty in getting back onto the road. One problem seemed destined to be replaced by another. Lionel was taking Ruby home each night and taking longer and longer. Also Claire noticed that when he arrived back home he kissed her hello on the cheek. That was not like him, and inevitably the horrible suspicion came over her that he was being unfaithful. There seemed to be no other explanation. She tried hard to dispel these unwelcome thoughts, Ruby was as nice and as friendly as ever and they were even close chums. On the other hand, Lionel did not seem to be quite himself – maybe it was all the extra strain of her illness – yet somehow the feeling that something was wrong kept niggling at her.

Then it all happened. Claire was finally fit and well again and finished with the hospital except for a check-up due in a few weeks' time and accordingly, Ruby spent her last day with her. Ruby's car was still mysteriously out of action and after the usual goodbyes, Lionel took her back home, presumably for the last time. When he finally returned his face was grim and full of emotion. He was clearly very uneasy.

'Oh, darling, what's wrong? You haven't had an accident, have you?' asked Claire.

'No,' he replied, it's just . . .' He clearly had difficulty in finding the right words. Claire could not help voicing her suspicions.

'Something to do with Ruby, is it? You've always been a long time in taking her home at night,' she queried, now with some anxiety in her own voice.

'Well, yes, Ruby and I . . .' He still had difficulty in expressing himself.

Claire jumped in with both feet.

'You're a weak man, Lionel, where women are concerned. I think she's taken you over.'

'That's it,' he almost whispered. 'She has – I'm going to live with her and I want a divorce, Claire.'

Claire was stunned and very confused. Did she hear right? This was her husband with whom she had lived happily for so many years. She looked at him in consternation.

'I thought you said you wanted a divorce,' was all she could say as tears began to form.

'I do,' he confirmed. 'But I feel terribly guilty about it. You've been a wonderful wife to me.'

Claire tried again through her tears, 'If I'm so wonderful, however can you desert me? You're not really serious – you can't be. It was not so long ago that you were lecturing a girl on your staff that it is not right to interfere in other people's marriages, now you must have encouraged Ruby to do it. How dare she break up our home.'

'I know,' he said. 'It all seems wrong, but I really can't help it. I've said I feel guilty and I really do.'

Claire was still in tears. Then, 'What about Philip?' she asked.

'Oh, he's old enough now to be able to take things like this in his stride,' was the rejoinder.

Claire could hardly believe her own ears. How could he care so little for his own son? She was sure Philip would be devastated. This was a despicable characteristic her husband had shown on occasions recently. Now his association with Ruby seemed to be making him worse.

'Oh,' she said. 'I thought you cared deeply about your own son.'

'I do,' he replied. 'You know that, but we've got to move on. Philip will be able to visit Ruby and me whenever he likes. We're going to live in Ruby's flat for a start. You know he gets on well with Ruby.'

'I wonder what he'll think of her when he knows she's stolen his dad,' said Claire.

'I'll still be his dad and I'll still be around. It's no use worrying. We'll sort things out,' Lionel replied. 'I still love you and Philip, Claire. You'll always be in my thoughts.'

'Even when you're in bed with Ruby – I doubt it,' she replied tartly.

'What's done is done,' he replied quietly. 'I'll see that you're all right financially and I'll deal with all the legal stuff. Don't worry about that. I've had enough. There's nothing you can say which will make me change my mind. I'm off to bed. If you like, I'll sleep in the spare room and go early in the morning.'

'Do,' replied Claire, 'and leave me to tell Philip, I suppose. I'd better save that until tomorrow evening.'

So they parted. What a shock! Never for a moment had she ever thought that such a catastrophe could occur in her life – it always happened to somebody else. How was she going to cope without Lionel and whatever did her future hold? She was unable to stop her tears from constantly welling up so could hardly sleep all through the night.

Morning came and a wearied and heartbroken Claire slid out of bed, dressed and went downstairs to prepare Philip's breakfast. Down he came, full of beans and hungry as usual. Claire looked at him wistfully. Little did he know that his beloved father was leaving the nest. How she was going to get through the day, she could not imagine. She must tell Pearl at least, Pearl would be comforting. The boy interrupted her thoughts.

'Where's Dad,' he asked.

'Oh, he had to go to the office early,' she replied, hoping that the boy would not be too inquisitive, she just could not tolerate spreading the sad news yet.

'He didn't say goodbye to me,' the lad said. 'And you don't look well again, Mum.'

Claire was desperate to smooth things over.

'Could be that he thought you'd be asleep,' she suggested. 'Me? I'm just a bit tired, that's all.'

The boy seemed satisfied with the explanation, had his breakfast then went off to school.

Claire breathed a sigh of relief, busied herself tidying up and then at mid-morning rang Pearl.

'Hullo Pearl,' she said when Pearl answered the phone. 'Coming along for coffee? I've got lots to tell you.'

'Good or bad?' asked Pearl.

'Well, very bad really,' answered Claire, 'but please come. I must talk to you. I'll tell you what's happened over coffee.'

'Right, I'll be along straightaway. See you' was the rejoinder.

Within a few minutes Pearl was there. Coffee was ready and they sat down together on the settee. Pearl started the conversation.

'I can't wait to hear your news,' she said. 'But you said it was bad, didn't you?'

'Yes,' answered Claire, 'the worst. We're getting divorced. Lionel has already left me.'

Pearl nearly spilt her coffee. She looked aghast.

'But I thought . . .'

'That Lionel and I would make old bones together?' interrupted Claire, feeling a little more relaxed now that she could talk about it to Pearl. 'He hit me with it last night.'

'Not that nurse you had?' queried Pearl.

'Yes, the rotten bitch,' replied Claire, 'posing as my helper and all the time working it so that Lionel had to drive her home at night.'

'But I thought that she had her own car?'

'She did, but it went in for repair and mysteriously enough it never came back – that's when Lionel started taking her home at night. I couldn't go with them with two plastered legs so he had her all to himself. I think they sometimes did more than just say goodnight.'

'God, how awful,' said Pearl. 'What a rotten sod Lionel is. Personally I've never really trusted him. He is a bit too sharp and nasty at times. But I never would have thought this would happen. I've always considered him to be at least the faithful type. Would you ever have him back?'

'No, I just couldn't,' replied Claire. 'Anyway, Lionel's not the sort. He would never admit his mistake.'

'I know, he's a pig-headed devil from what I've seen of him,' said Pearl. 'I'll bet you feel terrible. I'm so sorry, Claire.' She took Claire's hand and held it tightly. 'Is there anything at all I can do apart from keeping an eye on you?'

'No, I'll be all right – I hope,' replied Claire. 'Lionel's going to look after me financially and, of course, Philip too.'

'He bloody well ought to,' said Pearl fervently. 'Hey, wait a minute – if that nurse is working for a nursing association, she must be bound by some rules about professional etiquette. She just can't run off with a patient's husband like this.'

'Well, she certainly has done,' replied Claire.

'Yes, but couldn't you let her employers know what she's done?' Claire shook her head.

'What's the good? Lionel would only hate me for doing it. He's been reasonably generous so far so I wouldn't want to spoil that. Anyway, I suppose she would simply work for somebody else or go self-employed. No, Pearl, I could ring the nursing association but I'm sure it would not really help at all.'

'I suppose you're right,' agreed Pearl. Then. 'How's Philip taking it?'

'He doesn't know yet. I'll tell him this evening. I'm not looking forward to it. He would never believe anything like this could ever happen to him.'

'But now it has,' mused Pearl. 'Oh dear, what a disaster. I really am so sorry, Claire. Now we are both on the shelf.'

'That reminds me, I mustn't keep talking only about myself,' said Claire. 'Is Henry coming up to scratch yet?'

'No,' replied Pearl. 'No change – takes me out when he fancies it, spends plenty of money but never mentions marriage – he's not even sexy, just a jolly nice chap. I know he's got no other girlfriends so I'll keep working on him.'

'Well,' said Claire. 'Keep at it. He can't resist you for ever. Good luck.'

They chatted further and Claire began to feel more confident. At least she had both Philip and Pearl and many neighbours who could not possibly condone what Lionel had done and would remain her close friends.

Accordingly, the rest of the day passed uneventfully until she drove to the school as it was the week of her turn to pick up not only her own son but also two other boys. In the car together the boys chatted without ceasing. Claire listened to them with pleasure, she still had her son, his education and this job of collecting the boys to cling onto. Once home, however, her smile had gone for she then had the unenviable task of telling the boy that his father had left home.

'Philip,' she started.

'Yes Mum,' came the automatic reply.

'Well Philip,' she continued. 'You know there are a couple of boys in your class whose fathers have left them . . .'

'Oh, yes,' he replied, 'Tomkins and Brown. Their dads have gone off – bit of a laugh really but I 'spose not for Tomkins or Brown.'

Then came the shock as she said, 'Well, yours has done the same. Your Dad no longer lives at home, here.'

The boy was clearly bewildered and overwhelmed. He looked down and remained quiet. Claire eventually had to break the silence.

'He's going to live with Ruby a few miles away.'

Philip at last found his voice.

'But why can't Dad stay with us? She's nobody.'

'It's his choice, Philip. But you'll be able to go over to see him when you want.'

'But I don't want to see that nurse. She's horrible to have let Dad do this. Will we be all right here?'

'Oh yes. I'm still married to him for a bit longer. You'll always be our son. It's just that your Dad and Mum will live separately.'

'Well, I think that nurse is a stinker,' he said. 'Why couldn't she have left us alone?'

It was clear that he was reluctant to accept his father's new partner.

'It's as much your Dad's fault as hers,' Claire reminded him.

'Don't care,' replied Philip. 'She has no right to take my Dad away.' Then after a pause he said, 'When I see Dad, I'll tell him what I think of him – and that nurse too.'

'No,' cautioned Claire. 'That won't do any good. We've all got to live together somehow.'

However, Claire secretly applauded the idea. It would be as well if Lionel found that even his own son was disillusioned with him.

So life went on but now on a new track. Came the first weekend when arrangements had been made for Philip to live for a day or two with his father and Ruby. Claire attempted to soften the blow and get things moving on an even keel.

'Your Dad will be calling for you in an hour or so. Put on a clean shirt and change your socks. You mustn't let the side down. Have a good time in your Dad's new home, won't you? Remember that your Dad loves you very much – and Ruby does too.'

Philip dutifully went off to get changed. By the time he was ready, Lionel had arrived to collect him.

'I would've come to you by bus,' the boy said but Lionel was having none of that.

'Oh, no Philip, we don't want you travelling on your own at your age. Anything could happen to you. Surely you prefer a ride in the car?'

'Of course he does,' added Claire, then to Lionel, 'You'll bring him back on Sunday evening, won't you? Don't be too late.'

'We'll look after him,' said Lionel. 'I've got some good entertainments planned.'

'Feed him well and bring him back safe and sound,' said Claire. 'Remember, he's my son and you've only got him on loan.'

Philip then gathered up his belongings and went out to the car. The argument continued.

'He's my son too,' retorted Lionel. 'The only change is that he's now got two mums. We'll keep things going like this. Surely I won't have to get permission to see my own son?'

'Of course not,' retorted Claire. 'I'm willing to play my part. But you must remember that it is you who have made life difficult for Philip – and for me. You can't easily turn a child off and on like this. I just hope he gets on well with Ruby.'

'Oh he will. Back on Sunday evening then,' called Lionel as he went out.

Philip was duly returned early on the Sunday evening. He seemed to have had a good time but also was glad to get back to his main home and Mum. Claire was naturally anxious to find how he got on with Ruby and it seemed that she had been most attentive, generous and kind. To a certain extent Claire was slightly disappointed to find that things went so well. Nevertheless, she thought, time would tell. And it did, after a few more weekend visits, it was clear that the rot was setting in.

'It's all so different there,' the boy explained. 'I even have to go to bed earlier and Ruby is not so kind as you are, Mum.'

'What do you mean by that?' his Mum asked.

'Well she's very strict at table and even checks my hands to make sure I've washed them. She's like that with Dad too.'

'That's because she's a nurse,' said Claire. 'Nurses have to be ever so clean to avoid germs and other infections.'

'Yes, but we don't do all those things at home here, do we?' he replied.

Claire had no real answer so just said, 'Well, it takes all sorts to make a world, Philip. The difference with us is that you wash your hands but I don't check them because I trust you.'

He was too tired to continue the questioning so had his supper and then went off to his room.

Claire had certainly missed her boy over the weekend. It was so lonely with neither husband nor son. This was something she had hardly ever experienced before. Now all weekends would probably be the same. The house seemed so large and empty – no wonder she felt depressed.

Anyway, she always had Philip back for the ensuing five days and it soon became evident that his love and affection were hers alone. In fact, it was not long before his true feelings were expressed.

'You've told me always to tell the truth, Mum. Well, I don't like it there. It's not fair that just because Dad left us, I should have to keep going there. I don't really like Ruby and I'm sure she now looks on me as a nuisance. I know Dad gave me that posh calculator last time but I didn't need it 'cos I've nearly saved up enough for one myself. I think he's doing it to keep me going there. They're so different there and I like it here with you best, Mum.'

Such an outburst from her unhappy son brought relief to Claire. Clearly his entire routine had been interrupted and he was not himself lately. She had met Ruby on several occasions when she herself was either collecting or delivering Philip for his weekend stay and in a way the two girls got on fairly well together even though deep down Claire despised Ruby for the way in which she had quite casually broken up the home. So gradually, Philip's visits to his other home became less frequent. Lionel openly expressed his disappointment but was unable to blame Claire because it was Philip himself who made no secret of the fact that he preferred his weekends with his Mum. Secretly, Claire considered that it just served Lionel right.

After this Claire saw little of Lionel and nothing of Ruby. Most transactions were done by post. Certainly Lionel kept his word with money for the basic expenses. However, to provide the little extras and to keep herself well occupied, Claire soon got herself into the sort of job she knew and loved. Scanning the local papers for situations vacant, she had come across one for a receptionist in one of the larger hotels in Porchester. She telephoned the hotel and because she already had experience in that type of work, the hotel manager immediately invited her for an interview. No time was lost and the following day the interview took place. The manager opened up the conversation.

'Good afternoon, Mrs Halliday. Thank you for coming so promptly. I've already had one or two applications for this position but I'm interviewing you first because you mentioned that you earlier held a similar position in the Imperial Hotel. Naturally I've had a chat with their manager and he recalls you quite well. I'm happy to say that he gave me a good report about you. He also mentioned that you were a pianist. Are you still one?'

'Most definitely,' answered Claire. 'I love the piano and I play regularly.'

'Your own piano at home, I presume?'

'Oh yes, I have a small grand my husband bought several years ago.'

'How nice. Are you OK with classical music?' he asked.

'Why yes,' she replied enthusiastically. 'I love most classical music, not all, of course. I can, in fact, tackle any piece.'

'Would you be willing to play in the hotel just for a short time each afternoon – in addition to your other duties? I expect we will be able to pay you an extra dress allowance because all eyes will be on you.'

Her face lit up and, 'I would love that very much,' she replied.

'Good then, Mrs Halliday. 'You seem to have the charm and personality we need. Will you join us? I'm sure we can arrange an acceptable remuneration. Perhaps you would like to talk that problem over with our accountant.'

This she did and the position of hotel receptionist was soon settled. She went home more contented that she had been for a long time.

Meeting so many guests and hotel staff again helped to take her mind off the recent disaster. Encouraged by Pearl, she was determined to make the best of herself and in her new job it was important to keep her hair stylish and be fashionable in her clothes, in fact to maintain her elegance just as the hotel manager wanted. With Pearl's help and her own strength of mind, she was able to avoid continually reflecting on the past, uncertain as to why it all happened and to what extent she herself was to blame. However, as Pearl often reminded her, it is no good pondering over what might have been. At least now she was her own boss and she found that work took her out of herself. Moreover, she was able to console herself with the fact that she could not have found a more satisfying and happy job. Secretly, perhaps, she was hoping that a new man would come along, just as exciting as Lionel used to be but certainly a little kinder.

Her fears for Philip decreased with time. She had feared the damage a divorce might do to him, especially in that he might miss the support of his father. She need not have worried, Philip seemed to have resigned himself to the new circumstances and, anyway, he had plenty of school homework to keep him fully occupied. Philip did not tell his Dad what he thought of him after all so overall peace and tranquillity were restored. Later on, since Lionel seemed determined to settle down with Ruby, divorce from Claire became inevitable.

Getting divorced was a most unhappy experience. Lionel had first convinced Ruby that he himself should arrange

Claire's legal affairs through the company's solicitor but very soon Ruby took exception to this so a solicitor not associated with the firm was engaged. Because grounds for dissolution of the marriage were well established in that Lionel was conducting an adulterous liaison with Ruby and was living apart from Claire, she was relieved that a court appearance was not required, also that custody of Philip was simply resolved. Furthermore, there was agreement on the periodical allowance Lionel would make her. It was not so much the legal formalities which had been upsetting, rather more it was the psychological effect especially in that once done it was irreversible. For Claire it was a great disappointment, wondering always why she had failed to keep her man – or, in more simple words, what had Ruby got that she hadn't? Claire had certainly experienced the short-lived nature of true happiness, especially when her mind went back to those wonderfully happy days just after Philip was born.

Lionel too was anxious for completion so that he could eventually marry Ruby, hence he was unlikely to have suffered to the extent his wife of many years did. But Pearl was a comfort, sitting up with Claire late into the night of the dreadful day when everything seemed so final. 'Thank goodness for Pearl, I've always got her and Philip,' seemed to be Claire's only solace for when on her own it sometimes seemed that hope for her future happiness was collapsing around her.

3

More trouble was on the way. Philip was then nearing his eleventh birthday and for nearly all of the two years following the break-up of his parents' marriage, he had been a well-behaved lad, bright, reasonably cheerful and apparently still concentrating on his studies. He visited his father and the new wife, Ruby, occasionally and they still gave him a reasonably good time but somehow something was lacking. In a way he was unsure whether he was coming or going – in fact, he was doing both. Both his parents did their best for him, especially his beloved Mum who, in fact, found him quite a handful now that his father was seldom on the scene. Nevertheless, Philip managed well but life was not as easy for him as when he earlier had his Mum and Dad together. Moreover, in his school class he seemed to have been demoted to the level of his two other fatherless classmates. He never was quite sure of Ruby either.

One day a letter arrived from the headmaster of Philip's school. This asked Claire if she would arrange with the headmaster's secretary to call in 'for a chat'. Claire was excited. This must surely be something to do with Philip's future. She had always thought of him as being rather special and had a feeling that he was doing very well at school. To find that her son was progressing satisfactorily would give her the uplift she so badly needed. At last something good was happening. Claire telephoned the secretary and so within a few days of receiving the letter she managed to get time off from her job and was ushered into the headmaster's study.

'Take a seat please, Mrs Halliday. I must apologize for bringing you here on what might seem to be a trivial matter and thank you for coming.'

Claire felt apprehensive. She was hoping so desperately that he had something special to say about Philip's future. Despite all the earlier domestic problems, she was confident that he had been able to rise above the family difficulties.

'Let me say first,' the headmaster continued, 'this may be nothing to do with your boy at all but here we're getting rather desperate.'

All Claire could say was, 'Oh.' She wondered what was coming next. It could hardly be about Philip's progress.

The headmaster went on. 'One, or perhaps more than one, of the pupils is conducting a practical joke on almost everybody in the school by creating explosions.'

Claire's eyebrows went up. This sounded ridiculous and was clearly something she had not expected to hear. It was interesting, however.

'Explosions?' she queried.

'Oh, no, not serious ones, they are perfectly harmless but annoying. Let me explain as best I can. It's all to do with chemicals so I've got most of my information from the science master, Mr Hounsom. It seems that someone, who incidently seems to know quite a lot about chemistry, is using a chemical substance which while being made is wet and harmless, but when it is dry it is explosive to friction. I rather doubt that you will be able to recall nitrogen iodide from your chemistry lessons.'

'I certainly can't,' said Claire. 'I've never even heard of it.'

The headmaster went on, 'No, I'm sure you haven't. Few people have experience of it or even know about it, for obvious reasons. It is certainly not something to be kept in the home. In fact, I doubt if it's kept anywhere – it's too unstable. Also it is not mentioned in any of our school textbooks, nor are the ingredients generally available. We ourselves apparently have a small amount of iodine in a jar in a small cupboard in the chemistry lab. and Mr Hounsom is sure that some has been taken, that's how he guessed what was happening.'

'But surely iodine can be bought from any chemist – or has

it gone out of fashion?' queried Claire.

'Oh, no, it's not the stuff you buy in a bottle for cuts,' the headmaster explained. 'Pure iodine is actually metallic, really hard stuff. Why we've got pure iodine Mr Hounsom doesn't know, we both seem to have inherited it. It has never been used and must be very old. In fact, there are a few other chemicals which also ought to be disposed of. Unfortunately, the cupboard is not kept locked but it ought to be and will be.'

Claire had to admit that her knowledge of chemistry left much to be desired.

'No,' she said, 'my chemistry has seen better days. What has this got to do with Philip?'

'Maybe nothing,' he replied. 'But I've got to stop whoever is at the back of this. When my people move along corridors or stairs their feet cause tiny explosions, great fun for the kids but not for the teachers. The trouble is that it cannot be seen, each explosive granule is so tiny. Perhaps "explosion" is too strong a word. I myself have experienced it and it is really a sharp crackling noise, nevertheless quite alarming.'

'You must be thinking Philip has something to do with it, otherwise I wouldn't be here,' suggested Claire.

'Not necessarily,' replied the headmaster. 'I've already interviewed the parents of two other lads but so far drawn a blank. Philip is the third on my list and I'm sorry to mention this but he is, in fact, the innocent victim of a marriage breakdown, which is always unsettling for boys of his age. For many lads the difficulties associated with their schooldays are serious enough but even more so when they stem from divided families. When parents divorce, school can become such an unhappy place for the child because he mixes with other children who have both a mum and a dad. Kids react in peculiar ways to this and it may be that in a way he's artfully getting his own back on society and enjoying the fun and mayhem as he does it. Please forgive me for intruding into your private affairs but I've got to find the culprit soon. On the brighter side, I must say that whoever is doing it is a clever little devil. Not only is he good at chemistry but so far has avoided exposure.'

Claire began to feel more composed. She was quite sure that her Philip was not involved. He was a good lad and certainly would not upset other people by playing tricks on them.

The headmaster went on, 'Oh, that reminds me, earlier we had problems with some of the inkwells. The ink seemed normal enough but after use the writing tended to disappear. Invisible inks are not new but we certainly have no need of them in this school. Great fun for whoever did it but hardly funny for the user.'

'Oh dear,' said Claire. 'I don't think Philip would be so naughty, but isn't there something the school could do to catch whoever is responsible?'

'Nothing at all,' came the reply. 'Boys stick together and it is considered very wrong for one to tell on another. I've spoken to all the senior classes but, of course, without success. Could you please have a look round at home? It is a long shot but if it does happen to be Philip, and please believe me, Mrs Halliday, I hope it's not, you might possibly unearth something. Will you do this for me?'

'Of course,' said Claire, confident that she would find nothing incriminating. To please the headmaster she added, 'I can at least search his room. It is a holy place, not normally one that I should pry into, but I can easily do it while he's at school.'

The headmaster again apologized for the inconvenience he was causing her and she took her leave and went home, although now feeling somewhat apprehensive about the whole affair. Suppose it was Philip, what would they do to him? She was also worried about what the headmaster had said about the unsettling effect on children when parents break up.

At home Claire immediately went up into Philip's small bedroom and began by searching through the various drawers and cubby holes, there was nothing. Then she started on the books and suddenly came across a small and very dog-eared one entitled *Chemical Magic*. Her heart sank. She opened the book to see what the contents were and to her added horror found that there was a chapter entitled 'Noisy Floors'. Then she found a second chapter entitled 'Inks that can be erased'. Now she knew that it was her own son causing chaos at school. Why, oh why, was it just a clever schoolboy prank or was it because, as the headmaster had indicated, there was no man about the house to guide him?

With these thoughts buzzing in her mind she set about preparing the evening meal. It was a neighbour's turn to collect her own two children plus Philip from the school so Claire had plenty of time to think about her own and Philip's future. Her first thought was to say nothing at all but then she reminded herself that this would be dishonest. Anyway, she would have to face the headmaster and tell him lies. No, that was wrong and not like her at all. She must face the problem head-on. Then the door bell sounded and the miscreant was home.

'Hullo, Mum, it's me,' was the well-known greeting.

Claire felt a wave of panic coming over her but she steeled herself to handle the problem efficiently. Much as she loved her one and only, discipline must come first.

'Everything OK at school?' she asked.

'Yes, Mum. I say, you don't look very well. Can I do anything? Let me put my books upstairs then I'll give you a hand.'

'No, wait,' she said. 'I saw Mr Roberts, your headmaster, this morning and now I want you to tell me all about this.' She held up the book, *Chemical Magic*.

'Oh that,' said the boy. 'You've seen it before.'

Claire was surprised and more than a little uncertain.

'How long have you had it and when did I see it?'

'You gave me the money for it at the Church jumble sale just after Christmas. It was only 10p because nobody else wanted it.'

She felt rather deflated. If only she'd taken more interest in the book she might have avoided the present difficulties.

'The headmaster is concerned about little explosions which keep happening and I see that this book tells you how to do it. Have you been doing this?'

'Not me, Mum. It has been great fun at school. We don't know who's doing it. Fancy you thinking it was me.'

She went on, 'The headmaster thinks it might be you because you're good at science. and I'm sure this book proves it was you. You don't normally tell your mother lies, at least I hope you don't. Come on now, I want the truth.'

'Mum,' he exclaimed, 'you don't really think I'd do a thing like that, do you?'

'No I don't' she said, and now she was bluffing, 'anyway we can easily find out because there will be fingerprints on the jar of iodine in the chemistry lab.'

Claire felt that her bluff was beginning to work but he stood his ground, although by now looking apprehensive.

'Oh, I expect that whoever did it would have wiped his fingerprints off,' the boy suggested.

'Apparently he didn't,' continued Claire. 'Now the jar has been removed for examination so it can't be cleaned. The fingerprints will easily lead to the perpetrator.'

He gave in – her bluff had worked. Although Claire did not feel right in telling fibs, she excused herself on the basis that in this case it was the right thing to do. Philip's face had now really fallen.

'Sorry, Mum,' he said quietly, with tears beginning to form, 'it was me, but it was only a joke really.'

'A joke?' she exclaimed. 'You've had the whole school in an uproar and Mr Roberts and Mr Hounsom getting desperate. And I suppose you were also responsible for the funny ink they had. I see in the book that iodine is also used in that.'

'Sorry, sorry. I didn't mean any harm. Anyway, I told Dad about it all last week and he thought it was a great joke.'

'He would,' agreed Claire. 'I might have expected that from him. Didn't he even warn you of the consequences? Didn't he even tell you that what you were doing was wrong?'

'Not really,' replied Philip 'but he did say I ought to be careful.' After a pause he added, 'You won't tell old Robby it was me, will you?'

He was clearly getting worried but Claire was not letting

him off because he had been secretive and telling her lies. In addition, the headmaster was expecting a report from her and she couldn't say Philip was not guilty for that would make her as much a liar as he was.

'I'll have to tell him,' she said. 'He is expecting to hear from me and I think he already guesses who the culprit is. Have you any of the stuff left?'

'Only a little,' he replied.

'Then you'd better let me have it. I'll telephone for an appointment to see Mr Roberts in the morning.'

Philip was now really worried.

'Mum, please don't go. I'll never do anything like this again.'

'I'll have to,' she replied. 'He's expecting me to make a report one way or the other. It would not be right for me to tell him lies.'

'Gosh,' he said in alarm, 'I wonder what old Robby will do to me. He wouldn't expel me, would he?'

Claire was not letting him off lightly.

'I suppose he might. What a disgrace that would be. We'll have to wait and see. Now let's have some dinner.'

A very dejected and sorrowful lad sat down to his meal.

A telephone call for an appointment the next morning brought Claire once again into the headmaster's study. Mr Roberts was looking pleased as he was sure that Mrs Halliday had some important news for him. The said Mrs Halliday did not look so happy. She had brought a difficult problem with her, especially in what was going to happen to Philip.

'Good morning, Mrs Halliday. Is it possible that you have some news for me?'

Claire felt very small in his presence, just as though she was the one who had been responsible for the mayhem – well perhaps in a way she was.

'Yes, Mr Roberts, you may have already guessed. I'm now convinced it was my son, and believe me, I'm deeply sorry.'

'How did you find out?' the headmaster asked. 'Surely he didn't confess? Boys don't do that, at least not in my experience.'

'Not at first,' she replied, 'but when I confronted him with this book, in the end he had to. I'm afraid I had to persevere, he did not confess at first.'

She handed him the book *Chemical Magic*. 'It's all there on page nineteen. I must admit that I told him a little fib. I said that his fingerprints would be on the jar so you would be able to check. That brought him to a confession immediately.'

'That was a very clever move, Mrs Halliday, and it worked so well. We could do with you on our staff,' he said as he thumbed through the book. 'No doubt about it, but look, this book was published in 1906. How did he get hold of it?'

'At a jumble sale. It was only 10p. Nobody else wanted it.'

He continued turning the pages.

'There's stuff in here which is positively dangerous,' he said. 'Oh dear, listen to this about the so-called magical explosive. It is most interesting. "It explodes spontaneously if dried in too warm a place", and here's some more, "even a small speck of the material will produce a sharp audible explosion". Your young lad has really been playing with fire. He'd better thank his lucky stars that he hasn't injured himself.'

Claire had not read that part of the book.

'It's really frightening, Mr Roberts,' she said.

'I agree,' was the reply. 'I'm sure no publisher would print such a book nowadays.' Then after more searching, meanwhile leaving Claire anxiously awaiting her son's sentence, 'Has he any more of the chemicals at home?'

'I've got them here,' replied Claire as she handed him a small jar. The headmaster looked at it.

'And the whole school upset by such a small amount of material. Still, I suppose all explosives are like that, small in size, but giants in output.'

Claire could contain herself no longer.

'What are you going to do to Philip? You won't expel him, will you?'

'Well,' he replied, 'the problem has been discussed by the staff generally and several teachers are rather annoyed about the whole affair, especially because the perpetrator has been clever enough not to get caught. They, would, therefore, willingly vote for his expulsion.'

Claire was alarmed.

'Oh dear, you are going to expel him then?'

'Well,' continued the headmaster, 'my feeling is that your lad is not deliberately disruptive and that's in his favour. He just seems to enjoy playing tricks on everybody more or less incognito. As I've said before, boys will be boys. We have to tolerate juvenile behaviour, as long as it doesn't get really out of hand. Unfortunately, in this case it has. At this age young Halliday misses the heavier hand of a father so we won't put all the blame on the boy. No, Mrs Halliday,' came the reassurance, 'this problem has not reached the school governors so it's in my hands really. I can easily win the staff over so I think you can take it that we'll keep him on. May I add that you yourself have been a great help. In fact, without your cooperation, this could have gone on until the iodine ran out. I am very grateful for your honesty and all the help you've given me.'

Claire breathed a sigh of relief. She considered it unwise to tell the headmaster that his father knew of Philip's misdeeds but did little to dissuade him. No evidence of a father's heavy hand there.

'I've thought a lot about it,' the headmaster continued. 'Generally children should be rewarded for good behaviour rather than being punished for wrongdoing but I can't have disruption like this in the school so he's got to be taught a lesson and the rest of the school must know. I propose having him on the stage at assembly while I explain to the whole school what he has done, or rather, because they all know about it, how he has done it. Then we'll give him some after-school exercises or lines to do – at home, if you don't mind, Mrs Halliday. If we kept him here after school, I would have to have him supervised and I've certainly no spare staff for that.'

Claire felt much happier.

'I'm very relieved, Mr Roberts,' she said, 'and I will do my best to keep him straight after this, I promise.'

'Believe me, Mrs Halliday,' the headmaster replied, 'as I've already indicated and, of course, you must know, it is difficult to produce a stable background for children living with only one parent. However, in spite of all that you've got a good intelligent lad there. All human beings arrive on this earth with different intellectual capacities and happily I can tell you that, in your son's case, he's very bright, and this is more than I can say for many of my pupils. Take heart from the fact that in my experience it is boys who underachieve at school who commit most real crimes and, in fact, it is these lads who tend to fill the ranks of the unemployed. Halliday is certainly not one of these, he's just a bit – no, perhaps more than a bit mischievous, that's all. No worries now, together we'll keep an eye on him.'

Claire got up to leave.

'Thank you for being so nice about everything, Mr Roberts. I'm just sorry that it was my boy – but I can assure you that he won't be up to playing such tricks again.'

As she got to the study door the headmaster called, 'You've nothing more to worry about, Mrs Halliday, except to see that he does his task each evening, probably for no more than a couple of weeks. I'll have him in my study later in the day and read him the riot act.'

When Philip arrived home that evening it was quite evident that he had been up before the headmaster. He certainly did not seem to be his usual hungry self.

'Mum, why did you have to tell old Robby? D'you know, he's going to tell the whole school about me at assembly tomorrow?'

'Yes, he told me what was going to happen to you,' replied his Mum. 'You know, Philip, you just can't play tricks like this, upsetting the whole school. You've had your fun, now you've got to pay for it. I'm not sorry for you, you've really been a bad lad and I think old Robby, as you call him, is letting you off lightly. Whatever made you do it?'

'Oh it seemed good fun and some of the other boys

thought it was a clever trick.'

'Well, no doubt it was clever, but look what a fool you've made of yourself.' Claire could not let him get away with it. 'You could even have affected your future by getting expelled and that would have brought disgrace on us. Thank goodness that Mr Roberts agreed not to do this.'

'Gosh, Mum, would he really have done that?' Philip said, not without some alarm. 'Where would I go?'

'He could have expelled you to teach others a lesson but we talked it over and he could see that I would be very upset so happily you stay on. On the more cheerful side, he thinks you are a good worker with promise – but provided that you don't play any more silly tricks.'

'Of course I won't, Mum,' he replied. 'Come to that, I don't really know why I did – 'spose I wanted to let some of the other chaps see how clever and daring I was.'

'They won't think you're a clever lad after assembly tomorrow,' answered Claire. 'Don't you dare do anything like that again. And I'm disgusted with your father for not telling you what a fool you'd be. He ought to have stopped you before you got too involved.'

'Sorry, Mum, honest I am.' he said contritely. 'Dad does seem to have let me dig a big hole for myself. I s'pose he ought to have told you. Promise I won't do anything like this again.'

'Good. You'd better not. Now are you hungry?' she enquired.

'Yes, Mum. I'm OK now. What's to eat?'

At school assembly the next morning Philip experienced a few moments of glory when he was named as the perpetrator of the recent disturbing exploit. His glory was short-lived, however, for he was called to the stage to stand by the headmaster while his punishment was announced. Then the whole school was lectured on the subject of getting down to the job of learning rather than playing the fool, also that the boy Halliday had narrowly escaped expulsion.

At this point Philip no longer felt proud of himself – what

made him take such a risk kept going through his mind. He'd been made to look a fool in front of the whole school. Yes, he'd promised Mum not to be so silly and daring in the future and he must keep that promise. The punishment? Well, he would soon get over that.

Home he went at the end of the day to an unforgiving but still loving Mum and, of course, that evening was spent in his room plodding through the task the headmaster had set him. The many subsequent evenings spent in the same way had the desired effect. Philip slowly realized that he was not such a clever lad after all.

4

Months went by, with Claire settling down to her new way of living. In her job as a hotel receptionist she was able to acquit herself with glory for the hotel had recently installed a grand piano in the main lounge. This was mainly for evening soirées but frequently also in the afternoons, when the lounge was full of guests, Claire would play some of her well-loved classic pieces and, of course, other requests, to the delight of all, especially the manager who continually complimented himself on his choice of receptionist. Because she certainly was attractive enough for people to notice her, she occasionally had the problem of male guests thinking that she would be anxious for a no-strings attached flirtation. In a way this gave her confidence that she was still wanted. However, she was determined not to form a new relationship until she was absolutely sure of herself. She also had to endure awkward attempts by friends and neighbours to pair her off.

Philip had truly learned his lesson about school pranks and he certainly appreciated the remark by Dr Johnson that 'Pride must have a fall'. Accordingly, he was getting down to his studies and being as nice a boy as he could to his lonely Mum. He was determined to help her all he could and Claire loved him deeply for it.

With the more practical hardware she had confessed several misgivings to Pearl for recently there had been trouble with both the washing machine and the car. Being a working girl, it was often difficult to arrange appointments for maintenance engineers to carry out repairs. Happily, the hotel manager was so satisfied with her performance in the hotel that he gladly allowed her the few short periods of time off for this. In a way, it actually improved her standing among the hotel staff for on the occasions when she was away, inevitably some of the regular guests would enquire after her, fearing that the music would be no more. Also with the car, for example, having to leave it for service with a garage left her completely reliant on public transport which, for those living in the country away from the town, hardly provided the most frequent of services. These two events alone made her realize just how much she missed the help and guidance of an efficient husband. True, help came from service organizations, but they had to be paid and she was not exactly overburdened with money.

Philip's visits to his father seemed to be getting more and more curtailed. Claire formed the impression that Ruby had lost all interest in the boy, and even his father seemed to be less welcoming. This was regrettable because Claire was beginning to miss their help during school holidays in looking after Philip while she enjoyed a few days of peace. It did seem that Lionel was not exactly having the life he had fondly anticipated. According to Philip, Ruby's work was such that she was often working late into the evening and she seemed to have no intention of giving up her job. Claire had expected them to have a happy event but, so far, none. Perhaps Lionel and Ruby did not intend to raise a family at all but if, on the other hand, they did, then it would have to be soon because Ruby, like Claire, was getting on in years.

Pearl and Claire often had cosy chats about themselves and their futures.

'You said you would never have him back – changed your mind at all?' Pearl had once enquired.

'Certainly not. It's much too late. He's not to be trusted and, anyway, Ruby's got him,' was the quick reply. 'Actually, Lionel's own father was a bit of a devil morally. It's most likely that he has passed that particular gene on to his own son. What about Henry?' she continued.

'Oh,' replied Pearl. 'No action so far. I think he's still going through the process of making up his mind. I'll have to give him a nudge soon.'

In fun they also discussed whether they would opt for an easy, safe married life or one with a man full of passion but hardly steadfast and dependable. No conclusion was ever reached.

So peace and tranquillity were restored – but not for long. A pessimistic writer of the eighteenth century concluded that, 'It never rains but it pours' and Claire was about to experience the full force of that remark. Arriving home in the late afternoon from her work a few days later, she entered as usual by the front door and to her horror saw that her beloved home had been burgled. She could hardly believe her eyes and for a moment felt quite faint so sat on a chair in the hall. She slowly got up and momentarily was puzzled because both front and back doors had alarms fitted. However, soon the burglar's entry method was revealed because a pane of glass had been removed from a kitchen window at the back of the house – a neat job indeed. This window looked out on the back garden and the open fields beyond. Evidently that was how he got in without being seen, just at the time when most neighbours were also away from home.

Now feeling a little better, she hurriedly looked round the rooms and started tidying them in an effort to assess what had been taken. Thank goodness we're well-insured, she thought. Her ex-husband had taken care of that. Happily, her home had hardly been ransacked. Clearly the burglar had done his thieving quickly, probably searching mainly for money, of which, luckily, there was little in the house. Bank and credit cards and cash were all with her in her handbag at work. Missing mostly were her jewellery and one or two small expensive ornaments.

Claire tidied up and then sat down, by now thoroughly depressed, suddenly realizing that she had not called the police. This she did and was promised a visit within a short time. Then Philip arrived home from school, delivered by her neighbour. It did seem that he was not as distressed as Claire had imagined he would be. In fact, this was rather exciting news to him. There had been odd occasions at school when other boys' homes had been visited by unwelcome rascals and now it was his turn. He would have lots to tell his friends the next day.

'What about the police, Mum?' he had enquired on first being apprised of the distressing event.

'They're on their way,' his mother told him. 'I don't think anything has been taken from your room.'

That brought him to heel. 'They wouldn't touch anything of mine, would they?' Then, on second thoughts, 'I'll bet he's taken my train set.'

'Go and have a look,' said Claire. 'He wouldn't take a thing like that. It's far too heavy. And what could he do with a model train, play with it?'

'The engine is worth a lot of money,' he called as he went upstairs. Soon he was back with the glad news that nothing had been touched in his room.

Then the bell sounded and Claire let in two plain-clothes policemen. She told them her story and they listed the main items Claire thought had been taken. They looked around, especially where the thief had entered the house.

'Pity the window wasn't double-glazed, Ma'am. That would have given him some difficulty.'

One of the men stayed talking to Claire while his colleague continued checking the rooms.

'Yes,' replied Claire. 'We've got the doors secured but double-glazing all round is a rather expensive job and I couldn't afford that at the moment.'

Then Philip could wait no longer.

'Aren't you going to search for fingerprints, sir?'

'Not worth it, sonny,' the man replied. 'This looks to be the same bloke who did your neighbour a few houses down the road, the Charlwoods if I recall the name correctly. He wore gloves. Couple of days ago.'

Claire was distraught.

'Oh dear, I didn't know that.'

'I'm very surprised,' the man answered. 'And your husband didn't know either?'

'No,' she replied. 'We're divorced – my boy and I live on our own. I'm at work most days, that's why I hadn't heard.'

'Oh, sorry, Ma'am. Well, there's not a lot more we can do here. But rest assured, we're after him. He won't get away for ever.'

'But if he's working around here, don't we get some sort of police protection?' asked Claire.

'Not a hope,' came the reply. 'We just haven't sufficient manpower. I know how you must feel but this one won't visit you again – he's had all your goodies. Well-insured, I suppose?'

Claire nodded in agreement. The two men then took their leave with a reminder that they could be contacted at any time.

Needless to say, the whole incident left Claire very uncertain and missing having a man about the house. That night she slept with her bedroom door open and got Philip to do likewise. Her son was not a fully-grown man yet but she found that somehow having him with her in the house was comforting.

Pearl was a great help too. She knew all about the break-in at the Charlwoods while her home had obviously been spared because her parents were there most of the time. She helped Claire to list the items stolen and together they completed the insurance claim. Claire decided not to bring Lionel into the affair for he was no longer part of her own life and there only remained the rather tenuous link of the house and their son, Philip.

Accordingly, as the weeks slid by, Claire settled down but always mindful of what had happened. She took comfort from the detective's remark that this particular burglar was unlikely to visit her home a second time. Pearl did her best to comfort Claire by becoming in a way more attentive. This resulted in their meeting for a weekly Saturday morning session in a particularly attractive *olde worlde* coffee shop in town. Claire thoroughly enjoyed these outings with Pearl, especially as she was not deserting Philip who was now always off doing his own thing.

Then came a day when, while sitting at a table chatting over their coffees, Pearl noticed a well-dressed man, probably of an age similar to theirs, watching the pair of them intently. She caught his eye and to her surprise he rose from his table and went over to theirs.

'Good morning, ladies,' was his greeting. 'Might I trouble you for the sugar. There isn't any on my table?' Then, 'I hope I'm not intruding but it is a bit lonely over there.'

They were a little surprised at his boldness and hardly knew how to handle the situation. Pearl spoke first by reassuring him that it was anything but trouble.

Then she added, 'Come and join us then, bring your coffee over.'

This he did, purloined a chair from an adjacent unoccupied table and sat down. 'You must think I've got a nerve, approaching you like this,' he said.

'Not at all,' replied Pearl, 'but what are you doing on your own on a Saturday morning? No wife or girlfriend?'

'Neither,' he replied, then with a twinkle in his eyes, 'I couldn't resist wanting to chat to a couple of pretty girls.'

'Oh, flatterer,' replied Pearl, then to Claire, 'Shall we accept him as our guest?'

'We'll have to, he's already here,' laughed Claire.

So the conversation continued until their consciences began to remind them that they ought to leave for a waitress was already hovering nearby, anxious to prepare the table for luncheon.

'Will you be here next Saturday?' he asked.

They nodded in the affirmative. 'May I join you then?' he pleaded, 'but please say no if you think I'm being a nuisance.'

'I've enjoyed your company,' said Claire. 'I'm sure my friend and I would be happy to see you again – yes, Pearl?' Pearl nodded agreement, then he said 'What a lovely name, and to Claire, 'Yours is?'

'Claire,' she answered.

'Two charming girls with charming names. I'm certainly looking forward to next Saturday.'

'I suppose you have a name too,' enquired Claire.

'I'm sorry, I forgot,' he replied. 'Yes, I'm Ronald – Ronald Jenner. I'm a salesman in the wine and spirit trade.'

At that they parted. On the way home the two girls naturally discussed their new-found friend at length. They both agreed that in a way he had everything: he was intelligent, good-looking, had a charming manner and was well-dressed.'

'He's all yours,' said Claire.

'No, I've already nearly got Henry,' answered Pearl. 'He needs some more work done on him yet.' Then she added, 'I'll let you have this one. You need him more than I do.'

Little did they know that the man's affection for Claire was already growing.

They enjoyed his company just as much on the following Saturday. He seemed to be everything a girl could want. During their coffee, now with cakes for he insisted on paying for it all, Pearl left to visit the ladies' room. Ronald turned to Claire. 'I think you're a lovely person, Claire. Will you join me in a visit to the cinema or somewhere?'

Claire was taken aback. It hasn't taken him long to make a move, she thought. She longed to say 'yes' but should she? Was he after more than she would be prepared to give? If she did agree, she was sure that Pearl would be happy for her.

'I have a young son,' she countered.

His reply surprised her.

'Bring him along too.'

So Ronald seemed to be genuine. He just wanted her company, nothing else – or was he playing a waiting game? Oh well, in for a penny in for a pound.

'All right, I'd love to,' she said. 'Here's my telephone number.'

Then Pearl came back.

'You both look like the cat who's swallowed the cream,' she teased.

'Ronald wants to take me out,' explained Claire.

'Good for him, you both need a break,' replied Pearl.

And so Claire and Ronald's association blossomed. Claire was not too keen on having young Philip tagging along so she usually managed to see Ronald when Philip was occupied away from home with his friends. Pearl joined in with them on Saturday mornings and generally a good time was had by all. At other times Claire usually met Ronald in town; because she lived some way away it seemed the obvious thing to do. Besides, she wanted to be sure of him before she invited him into her home. Hence it happened that he himself made the first move.

Emerging from a cinema one evening he surprised her with, 'Will you finish off a lovely evening, Claire, at my flat? No monkey business, I promise.'

Claire could hardly refuse, not that she wanted to, especially as Ronald already knew that Philip was staying with his father overnight.

'Yes, I'd love to, as long as I'm not too late,' she replied.

'Oh good,' he said. 'My flat is only about ten minutes' walk away, or shall we take your car? Mine's in a garage near the flat.'

'Let's walk, it will do us both good,' was Claire's answer.

So they walked arm in arm to his flat, a modern but compact abode. Inside he sat her in an armchair while he went into the small kitchen to make the coffee. Claire sat looking around her but then natural feminine curiosity made her get up and wander round the room looking at pictures and the few ornaments. A figurine on a side table caught her eye, it was a truly beautiful one of Lady Jane Grey. He came into the room with coffee on a tray as she was admiring it.

'Lovely, isn't it?' he said. 'Look at the colouring and the gold leaf on her dress.'

'Oh, I know it well,' replied Claire. 'I used to have one just like this. Do you know who she is?'

'As a matter of fact, I don't' he replied. 'I've only had it a short time.'

'But there should be a leaflet with it giving some of the history.' Claire continued while they were drinking their coffee. 'Actually, she was the unfortunate and innocent young girl who became our "nine days' queen" in 1553 after

Edward VI died. I'm not sure that I've got the date right but I do remember that the history books say that she was only 16 and that hers was the shortest and most pathetic reign in our history. She was beheaded soon after. A tragic story, indeed, and what a horrible end for a young girl. Did you know about it?'

'Thanks for the history lesson,' he smiled. 'No, I didn't know; what horrible things were done in those days.' Then, picking up the figurine, 'But she's lovely, don't you think? You had one then. Don't tell me you've sold it.'

'I never would have done that,' answered Claire. 'Actually, it was stolen.'

His face visibly paled and he seemed a little confused.

'Oh dear, how horrible. Did the police help?'

'No, there was nothing they could do,' she replied. 'They didn't even check the house for fingerprints. Actually, another house just up the road had been burgled earlier and the thief must have worn gloves. I assume that the detectives considered it to be the same man and that he would have worn gloves again. But the figurine was one of my treasures. It is in fact what they call a limited edition so there are not many of them around – mine cost several hundred pounds. Did you have to pay a lot?'

'Not really,' he replied. 'I got it at a car boot sale.'

'You what?' she exclaimed incredulously. 'Fancy one of these being at a boot sale. It must have been sold by a person who had no idea of the value.'

'Yes, I suppose so,' he said. 'So I was lucky to get it so reasonably, don't you think? I'm not sure how much I paid but I think it was under twenty pounds.'

'You certainly were lucky,' she agreed. 'To think what I had to pay for mine and you have actually got yours at a give-away price!'

Time was running short so they finished their coffees and he walked her back to her car.

At home, Claire, although she had enjoyed a wonderful evening with Ronald, could not get the figurine of Lady Jane Grey out of her mind. A car boot sale? It just didn't seem possible – yet, of course, it could be so. Somebody with no appreciation whatsoever of beautiful ornaments might have tried to raise a few pounds for it. But it still did not seem likely. You worry too much, she told herself but nevertheless without thinking why, she looked up in her diary the number of the figurine she had lost. It was 1297. This she copied onto a slip of paper which she put into her handbag. She actually felt a little guilty doing this. After all, there must be at least a thousand or two of these little statuettes about, so why shouldn't one come his way? With Philip already in bed, she fell into hers and slept soundly all night.

The evening out with Ronald was so successful that she readily agreed to another. Although Ronald had encouraged her to bring Philip along, she had avoided doing so – she had no misgivings because she so much wanted this man on her own. Moreover, Philip had his own friends. Accordingly, another happy evening out was ending in Ronald's flat and again he was preparing coffee. Claire's offer to make the coffee had been gently refused. As Claire sat in the armchair, her eye caught the bright and colourful figurine of Lady Jane Grey again. Something made her jump up, go over to it and look at the number on the base. To her great surprise and horror, it was 1297. So it was hers after all. She sat down again very confused and more than a little apprehensive.

He came in with the coffee, looked at her face, then said, 'Claire, have you seen a ghost? What is it?'

'Oh Ronald,' she blurted out, 'that's my Lady Jane – the one that was stolen from me. I just couldn't help checking the number on the base. It's 1297 and I've still got my certificate of authenticity to prove it.'

He was somewhat alarmed.

'You mean it was stolen from your home and now has found its way to me?'

'That's it,' she agreed.

They fell momentarily silent then he said, 'Let's have our coffee before it gets cold. Tell you what we'll do. I'm truly falling in love with you, darling. Will you accept it as a token of my love and affection?'

'I think I love you too, Ronald,' she replied. 'But you can't give me something which is mine already. We must tell the police. They might be able to trace things back from the car boot sale.'

'They won't,' he suggested.

'Why not?' she demanded.

'Well, I didn't get a receipt and I certainly can't remember the car number.'

'Couldn't we go to the next sale to see if you recognize the car?' she persisted.

'Not a hope,' he replied. 'It sounds like a good idea but I'm sure it wouldn't work. If we did catch the chap I'm sure he would deny everything.'

'Perhaps you're right,' she agreed. 'anyway, I must ring the police – the detective has left me his number.'

He was now clearly uneasy and said, 'But that would involve me. I don't want the police around.'

'Why not?' she enquired. 'You've nothing to hide.'

'Well, yes I have,' he said. 'Actually, I've got a police record.'

Claire was now really confused and disappointed.

'Whatever did you do to get that?' she queried. 'That's not like you.'

'Well, it was,' he replied, 'just something I pinched when I was very young.'

'But they can't hold that against you for ever, can they?'

'No, of course not. But it's better for me not to get mixed up with them, don't you agree?'

'I suppose so,' she said rather uncertainly. 'What do we do about Lady Jane then? I must at least let the insurance people know that I've found her.'

'Please don't,' he pleaded. 'It'll only lead to more trouble. Please let me give it back to you. It's yours so I don't want it any longer.'

'But,' she persisted, 'the insurance people will be paying me several hundred pounds for its loss – and now it isn't lost.'

'We'll sort something out together. When will I see you again?'

'Soon,' she replied. 'Give me a ring.'

They finished their coffees, walked back to the car and she drove home, her mind in a whirl. Just what was he playing at? This was something she had not expected and it was so disappointing.

Philip arrived home just after Claire. He quickly ate his supper and then went off to his room. That night in bed as he listened to his mother having a short session on the piano he thought 'Gosh, Mum's playing furiously again. I wonder what's upset her. It must be something terrible.'

Actually, Claire was endeavouring to console herself over something which she could not really understand.

Inevitably, Ronald telephoned a few days later and they again went out for the evening and walked back to Ronald's flat. Claire was rather thoughtful but he seemed to be in good spirits. Over coffee he chatted about anything except the subject she was anxious to explore. She herself made the first mention of the statuette.

'What about Lady Jane, Ronald?'

'Oh, no problem,' he replied. 'I've got her all packed up for you to take home.'

'Ronald, what is it really?' she persisted. 'You seem to be dead scared of both the police and the insurance company.'

'No, I'm not,' he countered. 'It's just that there's no point in going further – you've got your figurine back, there's no problem.'

'But there is,' was her reply. 'I will be paid for its loss through the insurance.'

'Let them pay you,' he said glibly. 'You are entitled to some rake-off after all you've been through.'

'Ronald, that's dishonest,' she exclaimed. 'You should know me better than that. No, I must tell the police it has been found. I promised the inspector I would contact him if anything at all came up. It might even help him trace the thief. Why are you so dead against my doing this?'

'Why don't we just let it rest?' he said. 'It's all over now, let it rest.'

'I keep telling you, I can't do that,' she replied. 'It just isn't right. Why do you keep opposing me on this? I'll definitely give the inspector a ring in the morning.'

'No you won't,' he countered, 'if you do, you'll spoil everything.'

'Rubbish,' was her sharp reply. 'I'll be doing the right thing and you might even get some compensation for your loss of the figurine – after all you've paid for it.'

'Oh darling,' he said, 'you've forced me into confessing. Don't you see – *I was the burglar.*'

Claire nearly spilled her coffee over the settee.

'Tell me you're joking, Ronald – you would never do such a thing.'

'I don't since I've been going with you. But I did and I enjoyed the risk and excitement. Besides that it was nicely remunerative.'

Claire could hardly believe her own ears. She felt sick at heart and was near to tears.

For a little while she was unable to answer him, then 'Why did you keep this particular item instead of selling it?'

'I could not easily pass it on because of the numbering in the base, also I rather liked it myself,' was his reply.

'And all this time I've been going around with a burglar,' said Claire eventually.

'No,' he countered, 'as I said, knowing you has convinced me that there is a better way of life. I really have given it up – you have before you a reformed man.'

'I see it all now,' said Claire. 'If I took any action, they would soon come and get you.'

'You're dead right,' then anxiously, 'you're not going to let this go any further, are you?'

Claire did not answer, she was so confused, then, 'Have you really given it all up?'

'Yes, honest,' he said.

To which Claire could not help adding 'Honest – that's a peculiar word for you to use.' Then after another pause, 'I'm so confused, take me to the car – no, on second thoughts, I'll go alone.'

'When will I see you again?' he asked as she went to the door.

'Give me time,' she answered.

'At least can I have your word again that you'll not contact the authorities,' he pleaded.

'Yes, I suppose so,' was her answer as she left. She even forgot to take the parcel containing her precious Lady Jane Grey.

At home, Philip again found his Mum withdrawn and unhappy. But he was very tired, went straight to bed and soon fell asleep. Claire on the other hand had a rather sleepless night. Whatever was happening to her? – it seemed that everything she touched nowadays went wrong. No, that was hardly true, she had Philip who loved his Mum, was now doing well at school and behaving himself – it was unlikely that there would be any more pranks. There also was Pearl, a staunch and loving friend – she could always rely on Pearl. She would ring her in the morning and tell her of the latest complications. No, there wouldn't be time then, her job came first and, incidentally, being on duty in the hotel might take her mind off her problems. She finally fell asleep but it was a troubled night.

The next morning however she was awakened by Philip shaking her gently.

'Mum,' he said, 'you've overslept. I heard the alarm but you must've slept through it.'

Claire immediately jumped out of bed, quickly prepared breakfast and off went Philip. She herself had only just sufficient time to get to her work, so, in fact, as she had expected, there was no time left to ring Pearl. This she did immediately on arriving back home in the afternoon. Pearl was at home so was able to join Claire immediately.

'What's it all about?' Pearl enquired. 'You seem quite desperate.'

'I am,' replied Claire. 'Pearl, I'm in a mess, a terrible one. Ronald Jenner is a burglar – and he's the one who did this house.'

'Oh, that can't be true,' answered Pearl, 'he must be pulling your leg – having a bit of fun with you.'

'No, it *is* true,' said Claire fervently, 'he has already admitted it.'

Pearl gasped then said, 'No, I can hardly believe it. He seemed such a gentleman.'

'Maybe,' added Claire, 'but even a gentleman can be a thief. To think I was falling for him – and he still wants me. He's promised to be a good boy in the future.'

'That's a fat lot of good,' answered Pearl. 'However could you sleep easily in your bed next to an ex-burglar? Well, what has happened?'

'Oh, Pearl, you know that beautiful figurine I had of Lady Jane Grey, well he had one and when I checked the number on the base, I found it was mine. I wanted to go to the police and that upset him because apparently he has a police record already. Then when I persisted, he had to confess that it was he who burgled this house. In fact, some of his money might have come from selling my stuff – isn't it odd that in a way I've been the one paying for him to entertain us. I've promised not to do anything at the moment. It will mean prison for him if I do and I'll have my Lady Jane back and still be paid for it by the insurance people. That would make me as much a thief as he is.'

All Pearl could say was, 'Oh dear, what are you going to do then?'

'That's it,' said Claire. 'I don't know. I just do not know. Help me, Pearl, there must be some way out of this mess. I just don't want to be responsible for his going to prison – would you?'

'Well, I would,' said Pearl, 'because he's also burgled other people. I'll bet he also did the Charlwoods. But I've not been emotionally tied up with him as you have so I can understand your reluctance. No, if I were in your shoes, I don't think I would shop him. I say, why not leave the statuette with him and say nothing. Wait, here's a better idea, have the statuette back and advise the insurance people that it has turned up – we could easily think of some excuse.'

'Oh, you are a dear,' exclaimed Claire. 'I've been so upset

and confused, I haven't been able to think straight.'

'I know the feeling,' her friend replied. 'Shall we do that?'

'Yes,' said Claire. 'That seems to be a way out. He had packed the ornament up but I suppose I was so upset that I forgot to bring it. I'll bet he'll be over with it. But I can't tell the authorities about him, I really can't. I know I'll feel guilty about it for the rest of my life.'

Claire was right. Later that same evening there was a telephone call from Ronald. Could he visit her to deliver the statuette? She had to say yes because she needed it to proceed as she and Pearl had decided.

Then to her surprise he asked, 'Which is your house?'

That's an odd question considering that you've been here already,' she replied. 'I suppose you've visited so many houses around here.'

'No, that's not true,' he countered. 'It couldn't be more than two or three. But I don't know which is yours. Please let me see you again.'

What a mess Claire was in. She couldn't help liking the chap, she had even thought that she was in love with him – yet how could she continue the relationship, even though he had reformed? And for how long would that be? For a moment, she thought of refusing to see him, although he would obviously find her address from her telephone number and be along anyway – no, better to get it over and get Lady Jane back. Accordingly, she gave him her address and to her surprise he was there in just over half an hour. She let him in, he handed her the parcel and then sat down.

'Thanks,' she said, then 'I don't know why I'm thanking you, this *is* mine.' More jokingly, 'presumably you've removed all your fingerprints.'

'As a matter of fact, I have,' he replied. 'No self-respecting chap of that profession leaves finger prints around.'

'You call it a profession?' Claire queried. 'You said *that* profession as though you really have given it up.'

'I intend to, completely – if you will have me.' he pleaded.

'Ronald,' she exclaimed. 'I just couldn't live with you, knowing what you've been doing. I do like you and we did get on well together, but things are very different now. However, I'll keep your secret, I promise you that.'

'You've really made up your mind then. I suppose in a way I can't blame you. For my part, I feel I've lost something precious – and it's all been my fault.'

'I've lost something too,' said Claire. 'But we could never live happily together with this cloud hanging over us. And how do I know that you wouldn't return to your old habits later on? You must know others doing the same thing and there's somebody busy getting rid of all the stuff you steal.'

'You have my word,' he replied but Claire was not impressed.

'It wouldn't work – it just couldn't work,' she said.

Accordingly, after a cup of coffee he left and another phase in Claire's life was ended. It certainly had been a most difficult and harrowing one and her world seemed to be collapsing around her. She went to bed that night a very despondent and tearful lady. Could it be that she was already on the shelf and destined to be an old maid? Oh dear!

5

For weeks Claire struggled to get back to some sort of normality. Philip seemed to be developing well academically, especially in the subject of his first love, chemistry. He was still fascinated by his book *Chemical Magic* which had earlier led him to disaster but, fortunately perhaps for Claire, most of the chemicals required were no longer freely available from chemists' shops and certainly not to be stolen from the chemistry laboratory at school. Philip could, therefore, only dream of the fun he could have had were he around in the early 1900s.

Claire buried herself in her work. There she was bright, cheerful and a great success. At home in the evenings, however, especially when Philip was out, she felt anxious and sad. Thank goodness for Pearl, she often thought. She's been a brick. Whatever would she, Claire, have done without her? Ronald did not telephone. Claire half-expected that he might do so but he must have realized that he had made a mess of everything. She wondered whether now he really would give up his thieving ways or return to them. At least she had made him think seriously about his way of living. Oh well, that was his problem, she had plenty of her own to worry about.

Pearl, on the other hand, was beginning to blossom. Her parents had worried that staying too much at home because of her father's disability was holding her back. They had insisted that they could manage with perhaps a little help from a good neighbour if necessary. Pearl had, therefore, looked around for a suitable job and had been accepted as a sales assistant in an up-market dress shop in the local town.

However, she was to be more than this. As a tall girl with a good figure and presence she would also model dresses when required by customers and again on special occasions when the public were invited to a dress show.

This new job did much for Pearl for as part of her job she had to be well and tastefully dressed and as she put it to Claire, 'tarted up'.

Such was the shapely elegance of the new poised and sophisticated Pearl that her so-called boyfriend Henry began to sit up and take notice. Either he had begun to realize what an attractive girl he was courting or, alternatively, he might have been concerned that somebody else would beat him to it. Pearl naturally hoped that it was for the former reason but, whichever it was, he proposed and Pearl was over the moon. She had brought him to heel at last. Accordingly, she had plenty to talk over with Claire.

One of Pearl's first reactions concerning her future marriage to Henry was the change of her name.

'Fancy,' she said to Claire,' 'I'll be Mrs Pearl Reardon-Smythe. Don't you think it sounds posh? You must meet Henry soon, you'll like him, bit on the slow side but I'll soon sort him out and get him moving.'

'I'm sure you will,' said Claire.

Then Pearl chattered on, 'He's an old dear really and I do love him. I'm sure he loves me too. He must do, otherwise he wouldn't have popped the question.'

'What does he do for a living?' enquired Claire. 'He's certainly got an expensive car so I suppose you'll be well off.'

'I think so,' answered Pearl. 'He's something to do with investments in London – you know, the Stock Exchange in the City. He deals in stocks and shares and that. He's also always talking to his colleagues about Wall Street – you know, the American lot.'

'Oh, is he?' said Claire. 'I know so little about that sort of finance. The weekly housekeeping is about all I can manage. Lionel was experienced in that stuff so I never had to bother.'

'Talking of that old rascal,' said Pearl, 'how's he getting on? Do you hear from him at all?'

'Not really,' replied Claire. 'I get most of my information from Philip. He used to go to see his father regularly but he only goes occasionally nowadays.' With a smile she added, 'of course, he loves his Mum more. I've met Ruby on several occasions when delivering or collecting Philip on his weekend visits. We get on quite well together but, frankly, I can never get to actually like her when I think about what she has done to me. She's a rotten thief really, stealing my husband as she did. I know you'll say that it takes two to tango and Lionel is equally to blame, but somehow I put most of the blame on her. But nowadays I feel I'm no longer full of anger and bitterness. What's the point anyway? It only detracts from my own personality.'

'I guess I know exactly how you feel. I'd be the same,' said Pearl.

Claire continued, 'I've read that second marriages tend to have extra difficulties. Lionel's main problem seems to be that Ruby is a bit of a gadabout whereas he, as I remember well, is of a more serious disposition. But I know little about them now, nor do I care. Let's talk more about Henry instead. Are you quite sure he's what you really want?'

'I hope so,' replied Pearl. 'He does seem to be a bit of an old fuddy-duddy but he can't be when you consider his job. Anyway, I'll get him going.'

'It ought to be easy, Pearl,' said Claire, 'you're a most attractive young lady. Any man would be glad to get his hands on you.'

'As long as it's only Henry, I hope you're right,' replied Pearl. Then, 'But what about you, Claire? Good looks and smart and look what happened to you. I've seen Ruby a few times and she's not half as attractive as you are. Anyway I don't think Henry's the sort of chap to wander off once he's married, I'd kill him if he did.'

Claire changed the subject.

'How long an engagement are you planning?' she asked.

'Practically none. I'm going with Henry next Saturday to choose an engagement ring and I think we'll be married in a couple of months. Now he's popped the question he can't wait any more than I can.'

'Where will you live then?' asked Claire.

'Oh, Henry has a nice house several miles from here on the other side of the town. He's going to show it all to me next Saturday after we've bought the ring. He has talked about moving nearer to London but that's only talk at the moment. He has a housekeeper at present. I love my job so I'm not going to give it up yet. Henry agrees so he might ask his housekeeper to stay on.'

Claire was becoming alarmed.

'You'll be gone right away, Pearl. I shall miss you terribly. You've been such a comfort to me all through my recent troubles.'

'I know,' Pearl replied. 'I worry about that too. But we both work in Porchester at the moment so we can still get together for coffee and a chat. We'll be friends for ever and ever – remember the solemn oaths we made at school?'

'Oh, yes,' replied Claire. 'You are and you always have been a great comfort to me, Pearl, especially since Lionel left. I hope I have been the same to you. It's just that it is so nice to have you near me. Still, I suppose Porchester isn't that far away so we can meet often.'

Pearl squeezed her hand.

'We will, Claire, we will,' she said.

So Pearl and Henry became engaged on the following Saturday. They then planned to marry as soon as possible.

'He's just woken up to what he's been missing,' Pearl had told Claire. 'Come to that, so have I. Henry wants to do everything properly so the banns have to be arranged next. We've decided not to go overboard but I am going to be married in white. I think I'm really entitled to do so because I've checked up,' and here a mischievous smile crept in, 'and as the dictionary expresses it, I'm morally and spiritually pure. Wouldn't you agree?'

'Because you're my best friend,' answered Claire, 'of course I agree – but I don't know what you get up to when I'm not around. When are you getting your trousseau?'

'Very soon, and I'm lucky because I get a good discount at our shop. I've actually modelled a few bridal dresses so I already know what choice there is. Tell you what, will you pop into the shop soon and help me choose finally?'

'I'd love to,' answered Claire.

And so it happened. The very next day at lunchtime Claire called in the shop and she and Pearl had fun with Pearl trying on the various white wedding dresses. One or two were rejected immediately but finally both were agreed on one which Pearl said happened to be chosen by many brides-to-be, full length in white satin with three-quarter sleeves and low neck. Pearl was overjoyed with Claire's choice because, in fact, this happened to be the dress she would have chosen for herself.

Claire did her best to be happy for Pearl but underneath sadness was growing as she recalled her recent disaster with Ronald, coupled with the fact that she would in the future see less of her best friend and close ally, also that her one and only son was growing up and might soon be leaving the nest. There is no doubt that underneath, Claire was having a difficult time. She seemed to have been left behind.

Nevertheless, her troubles were put on one side at Pearl's wedding. It was a happy time. Pearl was resplendent and radiant in her dress while Henry looked every inch the gentleman he was in his top hat and tails, not actually his, but hired for the occasion, Pearl had admitted. Claire was suitably dressed in her finery with Philip in his best bib and tucker. They made a personable pair, attracting many glances. Philip had not attended a marriage ceremony before and was sufficiently engulfed in the flow of the church proceedings that he was unexpectedly quiet during the whole time. Eventually the couple were at the church door for the inevitable photography session. Claire felt so happy for them even though, in fact, Henry was taking Pearl away.

The reception was relatively quiet at a nearby hotel. Pearl did not seem to have many guests, mainly because for years she had been more concerned with her parents than with friends. Neither were there many relatives. Henry, on the other hand, had invited quite a few professional colleagues with their wives in addition to his relatives. When he met Claire at the reception he had a grin rather like a cat which had just swallowed the cream and he was clearly enjoying every minute of life with his new-found partner. He certainly got full marks from Philip whom he had previously classed as 'an upright and good-looking young man'. Pearl was still looking dazzling in her wedding dress and managed to find a few minutes to chat with Claire, her old and closest friend, and to introduce her to several of Henry's friends, some of whom even Pearl had not met before.

So it all ended with bride and groom off on their honeymoon. Pearl and Henry had supposedly kept their honeymoon venue a secret but, in fact, everybody knew that they were off to Sorrento, on the coast of Italy. Claire was so glad for Pearl but that night at home, after all the splendour, she was in the dumps again, feeling more alone than ever. Thank Goodness she had Philip and even though he was now often out with his friends, he was hers and always home at night. Claire's almost solitary condition was destined for change, however.

One evening, just after their meal and when Philip had retired upstairs to his room for a clash with the inevitable homework, the doorbell rang. She opened it to find Ronald, smartly dressed and with a small bunch of flowers.

'Can I come in?' he said.

Claire was taken aback at what she considered to be the cheek of the man. She opened the door wider and beckoned him in.

'I thought our relationship was over,' she said.

'I just couldn't help wanting to see you again. We got on so well together,' he replied.

She thanked him for the flowers and offered him a cup of coffee which he gladly accepted.

He almost repeated himself, 'You're such a lovely person, Claire, I had to come. Can we forget the past and start all over again – please, darling.'

'But, Ronald,' she replied with a smile, 'you're a thief and an old rascal – you can't expect me to fall head over heels for you. How could I live knowing that one word from me would put you in prison?'

'No it wouldn't,' he countered, 'that's all over.'

'But you stole my things.'

'Maybe, but you've got no proof – none whatsoever.'

'What about my Lady Jane figurine?'

'I've made sure that you've got it back. Now there's no evidence to prove that I ever touched it.'

'I see,' she said, 'you were not only a clever burglar, Ronald, but now it seems, also a very artful one.'

'It's not a case of being artful,' he countered. 'It's simply one of the skills of the profession. No respecting burglar would ever leave fingerprints behind. To do so would be equivalent to sending a letter to the police to tell them the name of the whodunit.'

Claire began to realize that she was losing the argument. but 'once a thief, always a thief' was the expression foremost in her mind.

'No, Ronald,' she said. 'You can't win me over that way. There's no question of our relationship continuing.'

'Is there someone else then?' he asked.

'Oh, I do have other admirers,' she said with tongue in cheek.

'Are you going with anybody seriously?' he queried.

'That's my business,' answered Claire. 'Look, Ronald, we did have much in common and there was a time before I discovered these terrible things about you when I really thought you were great. But it's different now. However could you guarantee your honesty for the future? If I'm not mistaken, you actually love it all, the excitement and the risk, I mean.'

'Well I did,' he said, 'but Claire, I honestly will give it all up if you will have me. We get on so well together.'

'Past tense,' answered Claire. 'We did get on well together but now you've spoilt it all. No Ronald, I cannot, I just cannot, go out with you – surely you understand that. Thank you again for the lovely flowers, but you must leave – now.'

'Nothing I can say?'

He was trying hard again.

'No, nothing,' she said firmly. 'Off you go, Ronald. That's the end of it. I'm as sorry as you are – you're quite a nice chap underneath but the fact is that I don't really understand you at all.'

She ushered him out and then sat down to ponder over the mess her life was in.

Weeks passed by with little exciting activity except for a few coffee sessions with Pearl after she had returned from honeymoon. She and Henry had apparently spent much of their time in a small but nonetheless desirable hotel overlooking the bay where they were able to enjoy to the full the Italian sunshine. They had excursions further afield to Pompeii, Vesuvius and Naples. Pearl had especially enjoyed the tour round Pompeii and was fascinated by its Roman history. Their guide explained that the Romans had carried out a prosperous trade there and as they could see, had built many beautiful villas. However, Mount Vesuvius had decided to end all that by suddenly awakening from its years of idleness and engulfing the nearby city with a hail of pumice and ash. Many had perished in the turmoil. Happily, excavation work had revealed much about the Roman way of life in the forum, the temples and the great open-air theatre. Of great interest also was the fact, as narrated by the guide, that young girls were shipped over from the coasts of Africa for a 'tour of duty' and returned to their homes when pregnant, as they eventually were. Those Romans certainly knew how to enjoy themselves. Vesuvius was apparently of less interest, the huge crater managing to blow out steam in one or two places only. Nevertheless, it was fascinating to have actually walked around in the depth of a huge volcano. Naples was a different matter, there were dress shops!

So Claire, try as the might to forget her troubles, had only her hotel work and her beloved son to keep her mind occupied and herself happy. When on her own she often felt somewhat depressed but managed to shake it off with the help of a little brandy. However, things seemed to be getting worse, eventually compelling her to have a chat with her doctor. She sat in his waiting room, building up sufficient courage to approach him and wondering what she was going to say.

He greeted her with, 'Good evening, Mrs Halliday. I haven't seen much of you since your accident, or come to that even of young Philip. You must've both been keeping well.'

'Yes, doctor,' she replied, 'we have. But I'm feeling a bit low and wondered if you could buck me up with a tonic or something.'

'Bit low, eh?' the doctor answered. 'What's been happening to you to bring this about? You're fully over your accident, I presume.'

'Oh, yes, doctor,' she replied. 'But did you know that my husband walked out soon after I had fully recovered?'

'Yes, I did as a matter of fact,' was the reply. 'He's transferred to another doctor in town.'

'Well,' she continued as she gathered confidence, 'as if that wasn't bad enough, I've had several other major problems to cope with on my own since and I feel that life is beginning to get me down.'

She then gave the doctor a brief resumé of her recent difficulties. He listened intently then checked her pulse rate and blood pressure.

'You are in a bit of a shaky state, Mrs Halliday,' he concluded, 'and most of it seems to be due to your enforced lifestyle and what has been happening to you. I'm not too sure that tablets will be of much help because they cannot affect the way you have to live. I would like you, therefore, to have a chat with a psychiatrist.'

Claire was most surprised and a little frightened.

'Surely I don't need a psychiatrist, do I?'

'Not in the way you think,' he answered. 'I know you've been having a rough time but I'm a little surprised at its effect on you. You are a very sensitive lady, that may be the problem. We must get you on the up and up. You'll like the chap I have in mind. He's Doctor Granville. I believe he's about your own age so you will be able to talk freely to him. He can then advise me as to what treatment can help. Will you see him? Remember, you don't have to but I would like you to discuss your problems with him.'

She felt uneasy about visiting a psychiatrist but she had asked for help so could hardly refuse it when it was offered.

'Why yes, doctor,' she replied, 'if you really feel I should.'

'Good,' and, handing her a piece of paper, he said, 'here's his secretary's number. She'll fix you up. Now don't worry, Mrs Halliday, Doctor Granville will give us good advice. He will write to me after he's seen you.'

So Claire left the surgery, still wondering why she had agreed so readily to see, of all people, a psychiatrist and therefore feeling that she had dug a large hole for herself. Whatever did she need a psychiatrist for? It was a disturbing thought. Nevertheless, she could not face her own doctor again if she had not done what he had advised.

Accordingly, Claire made an appointment to see Doctor Harvey Granville and within a few days was to be found sitting opposite him in his consulting room. Her nervousness soon abated for he seemed to be a friendly chap, certainly not a man for whom the word 'trendy' would apply. Overall, not a bit as she had expected. He was reading the letter from Claire's doctor. He looked up, smiled and shook hands with her, so putting Claire completely at ease.

'I have the gist of your problem from Doctor Andrews here,' he said. 'Slight depression. That sounds ominous. Do you yourself think that I can help?'

What a question, thought Claire.

'Well, Doctor Andrews must think so. I had thought that all I needed was some medicine to help me relax.'

He continued, 'I know you've told Doctor Andrews about your more recent problems. Do you mind going through them again with me?'

Claire recounted all the happenings in her life, starting

with her falling down the steps leading to the house and subsequent days in hospital. She tended to make light of Philip's misdemeanours, then spoke of her problems with the burglar, Ronald, at great length. As she recounted the various events, she herself began to feel that it all sounded so improbable, yet it had actually happened. Then on to her loss of an intimate friendship with her lifelong chum, Pearl, to the renewed appeal by Ronald and so to the present time.

She ended up with, 'I almost feel guilty in making such a fuss when, in fact, I have a nice home and a son who is doing quite well, especially at school.'

'Yes,' he said. 'But clearly there is a lot lacking in your life now, especially because you were happily married originally. So many things which earlier meant happiness have now been taken away from you. Presumably you are depressed because you cannot see light at the end of the tunnel.'

'Yes, I'm sure you're right,' she replied. 'I seem to have experienced so many problems that I even worry that there may be more trouble ahead.'

'Not necessarily, Mrs Halliday, you shouldn't think like that. You seem to be a person with high excitability of the nervous system. Put more simply, you are a most sensitive person – but that is good. Now, as you've said, you've got your home and a son developing well. You've also got a satisfying job and your health and strength. What about other interests – or men friends?'

'I do love gardening, especially roses,' she replied. 'No, I have no other men in my life at present.'

'That could be your main anxiety,' he said. 'You were happily married once and that was suddenly taken away from you. Then the subsequent experience with your burglar friend went the same way. It is an amazing, almost incredible, story. That you should actually be friends with a chap who had previously burgled your house is surprising enough but the fact that he thinks you would marry him is bordering on the ridiculous. Do you think you were in love with him at all?'

Claire was not really sure how to answer.

'Well I liked him very much but I suppose I was not actually in love with him. Then, on second thoughts she added, 'well, I might have been eventually – he was a real charmer.'

'Nevertheless,' he replied, 'you were very right to close down the friendship and you must not get mixed up with the chap ever again. There's something that Shakespeare said that I often quote in cases like this. I'll read it to you.'

As he said this he got up and went over to his well-filled bookshelves.

'Oh dear,' thought Claire. 'I don't remember much about Shakespeare. Hope he's not going to get too involved, otherwise I'll look rather ignorant.' However, she need not have worried.

'Here it is,' he said, thumbing through a volume of Shakespeare's plays. 'I've often needed to read this to patients to show them that their troubles are nothing new. It's in *Much Ado About Nothing*.

'If you meet a thief, you may suspect him . . . to be no true man: and, for such kind of men, the less you meddle or make with them, why, the more is for your honesty.' Later on it says,' . . . if you do take a thief, . . . let him show himself and steal out of your company.'

'How's that? Shakespeare telling you exactly what to do and, in fact, you've already done it. Good for you.'

Claire began to feel relieved and better. What a way for a doctor to treat a patient – by quoting Shakespeare. Still, it was encouraging to find that she had taken the right action with Ronald.

He went on, 'Undoubtedly many other people may treat you unfairly, they themselves can be selfish and even cruel. Don't worry, Mrs Halliday, you are clearly an intelligent person and attractive. It would appear that you have a lack of faith in yourself. Look forward to meeting your next husband and forget about the first one. Surely many eligible bachelors pass through your hotel?'

'Yes, they do,' Claire answered. 'You're right doctor. I realize I'm being a bit silly. I should never have got myself into this state.'

'Don't worry,' he replied. 'So many people get depressed when things continually go wrong. They may even feel resentful and angry. Instabilities in modern life lead many people into medical disorders. How else would a psychiatrist make a living? Is there anything else you want to discuss? No other worries?'

'No, I was scared of coming to see you but, in fact, now I am beginning to feel much better. I'm very grateful for the chat, or I suppose you would call it a pep talk.'

'Fine, Mrs Halliday. Just remember that it is not so important what happens to you as the way in which you react to it. Making the best of unfortunate and difficult circumstances is a major requirement in life, so think in terms of turning a minus into a plus and try to manage without the help of tablets. I will suggest to Doctor Andrews that things will settle down for you. Just ring my secretary if you feel the need for help in the future – but I don't think you will.'

Claire left after that. Mindful of the advice she had just received, she was determined to buck herself up and get on with her life. She felt wonderful. He certainly had done her a power of good, and all without medicine.

6

Still conscious of Doctor Granville's remarks, Claire got back to work and although nothing much had changed, she did feel better and less likely to fall into depression. She had met Pearl on a couple of occasions for the usual exchange of experiences. Pearl was settling down to married life and it was obvious that she and Henry were enjoying life together. Earlier, Claire was happily married while she, Pearl was only hoping to be. Now Pearl was the happily married one with the unfortunate Claire left on her own.

Claire found that she had a great respect for Doctor Granville. At first the idea of being examined by a psychiatrist had seemed a little far-fetched but now she was glad of his help. What he had said gave her the confidence she needed, hence now feeling much better and stronger for it. In fact, she later handled a work problem very well without getting depressed about it. It so happened that one of the hotel junior managers, a man somewhat older than Claire, had constantly made light-hearted advances to her, so becoming rather a nuisance. She was not particularly keen on him anyway, he just wasn't her type, moreover he seemed so much older. Claire had already had a few words with him about his attentiveness but got nowhere for his attitude was simply that he liked her and could not agree that he was being a nuisance in any way. Eventually she had a chat with the general manager and, to her surprise, found that her follower had been reported previously for similar misdeeds. Yet apparently he was a good worker and generally an asset to the hotel. However, the manager agreed that something had to be done, said he would talk to the chap and even threaten to move him to another hotel in the chain if his behaviour did not improve. Happily it did, nothing more was said and relationships were soon restored to normal.

So life went on with little change for the next few months. Then one afternoon Claire was quietly playing the beautiful grand piano in the hotel lounge, completely unmindful of what was going on around her, when she suddenly realized that somebody was standing behind her. She looked round and saw that, of all people, it was Doctor Granville.

'I love your music,' he said. 'It seems that when you play, you and the piano become as one. That was a piece by Chopin, wasn't it? I thought I recognized his work. am I right?'

'Yes you are. It is by Chopin and was requested by one of our regulars. He often wants me to play it – to keep him awake perhaps.'

'Do you play here often?' he queried.

'Oh, yes,' she answered, 'most afternoons at present. It helps the tea and cakes go down. I hardly expected to see you here.'

'Oh, I have an elderly patient who has been living in this hotel for some time. I don't need to visit her very often, only when she gives me a call. How are you now? Feeling better and without so many worries?'

'Oh yes,' she replied enthusiastically, 'seeing you did me a lot of good. I'm lucky, really, in having this particular job. I suppose you would class it as an emotional necessity and it keeps me fully occupied. I do love it and I meet many people. In fact, I've just met you again. I feel now that I'm managing myself much better.'

'Wonderful,' he said, raising his hands, 'I said that you didn't really need a shrink and now I'm sure I was right.' Then suddenly, 'There's a small exhibition going on in our local museum. It's a special one of aboriginal artefacts – are you interested in coming along with me sometime over the weekend? It won't be as boring as you might expect.'

This took Claire completely by surprise. Did she ought to

say 'yes'? She very much wanted to but was it the right thing to do?

'I thought professional people like you were barred from fraternizing with their patients?' she queried.

'Ah, I've thought of that already,' he said. 'That's easily sorted out – in fact, you did not become a patient of mine. You did not even lie on my couch.' With a smile he continued, 'We only had a friendly chat, remember?'

'Little did I know that psychiatrists could be so devious,' she said. Then she paused, 'Oh, I'm sorry, Doctor Granville, I shouldn't have said that. It was very forward of me.'

'Feel free,' he replied. 'I'm off duty now. Please call me Harvey – and I can call you . . ?'

'Claire,' she answered. 'My middle name is Rowena but nobody ever uses that.'

He went on, 'But Rowena is a lovely name. Anyway you haven't said you'll come?'

'I would like to,' she replied. 'Perhaps there will be some aboriginal pianos there.'

'I doubt whether there are any piano factories in the Australian bush,' he said and smiled. 'But that reminds me, I do love to hear you play. I had been listening for several minutes before something made me want to go over and chat up the pianist.'

'I hope you don't chat up all the pianists you see,' she teased him.

'Only this one. I recognized that it was you immediately. I just had to see you again.'

Accordingly, they arranged that he would call for her at her home early in the afternoon on the following Saturday. The arrangement suited Claire well because Philip would be enjoying, or perhaps *not* enjoying, a school cross-country run then.

On the appointed day, Harvey arrived well on time. Claire was thrilled to see that he had a luxurious car – 'he must be well off,' she thought. She herself was dressed for the occasion with full but tasteful make-up. He too looked the gentleman he was, with a smart grey suit and what she perceived to be a college or professional tie to match.

'Hullo, Claire,' was his greeting. 'I am Lord Granville's chauffeur. The limousine awaits you.'

'That's nice,' she replied. 'But I'd rather be escorted by the chauffeur than his lordship.'

And so she was. He drove to the museum, managed to find a parking place and into the museum they went. Claire was surprised. The exhibition was more interesting than she had imagined it would be – or was it because now she had such a pleasant and even exciting man to escort her? He was so attentive. She even hoped the tour round the museum would never end.

But it did and then he said, 'How about a snack. They have places known as restaurants around here.'

Accordingly, they went for tea and cakes at a nearby patisserie. However, it all had to end and he drove her back home and escorted her carefully up the steps to her front door.

'So these are the notorious steps which caused your accident several years ago?' he enquired.

'Yes,' she replied. 'You can see how steep they are. But I go so carefully now that I'm sure I won't slip down them again.'

At the door she found herself uncertain as to whether it would be right to ask him in but he anticipated this, said that he could not stay but could he take her out again.

'I've had such a wonderful time with such a pleasant partner,' he told her.

Claire happily agreed and for this received a short kiss on the side of her face and off he went.

Philip was not yet home so Claire had time to sit down and ponder over the afternoon events. This Harvey Granville was such a nice chap and he seemed to like her. In fact, he wanted to take her out again. But wait a moment, first an unfaithful husband, then a burglar, now could it be a married man? Eager though she was to enquire into his background, she had been unable to do so for fear of spoiling an exciting afternoon. Was he married? That was the inevitable question. However could such an accomplished and good-looking fellow not be? If so, what was he doing taking her out – and even suggesting a second outing? Doubts started to creep in – yes, she must ask him all those awkward questions. After all, he already knew every intimate detail of her life. Then the door burst open and there was Philip, running shorts and shirt as muddy as ever. Philip had never been very keen on cricket and football but nevertheless managed to enjoy both sports on occasions. Overall, he was not much of a sporting lad and definitely when the occasional cross-country run had to be tolerated his keenness was at its low ebb. He certainly could not understand why most other boys actually enjoyed themselves on runs, for as he had so often decided, they must have ached all over.

'Gosh, Mum,' he exclaimed, 'we've been miles and I was nearly last again. My legs ache right up to my shoulders.'

'Oh, go on, silly,' his Mum replied. 'Have a quick shower while I get something to eat.'

'What's for dinner?' he asked. 'Never you mind,' she replied.

Claire's desire to know more about her new-found friend was soon satisfied. On the very next occasion when they were out together she just couldn't help dropping the bombshell.

'Forgive me for asking, but are you married Harvey?'

'Oh,' he replied. 'I should have told you – no, I'm not.'

She was a little surprised but very relieved.

'I was married,' he went on, 'but it all fell apart many years ago. When I was leaving college I fell in love with a girl student who, like myself, had just qualified. We were mad about each other, so got married quickly. We both soon had jobs so were able to rent a small flat and everything seemed to be perfect. But somehow it didn't last. After nearly three years Peggy decided that she loved someone else more than she loved me. The final result, of course, was divorce. Believe me, I especially found the divorce procedure and final outcome most difficult and depressing. That's why I can appreciate what you yourself have gone through. However, Peggy and I did have a good life together while it lasted. I had continued studying and it may be that which she couldn't cope with – who knows? What a good thing we had no children. So, Claire, you and I are both in the same boat, once married and now footloose but I hope no longer fancy-free. That makes us both second-hand, so we've much in common.'

This revelation was all Claire needed. With him she felt she was somebody who really mattered and so she was able to believe in herself again, in fact, becoming a different person altogether. She also felt much more secure with him and now knew that she was not helping him to cheat on somebody else. Accordingly, their friendship grew and blossomed. Life in each other's company became less formal when with Philip they spent a day at the seaside. The sun shone and they arrived at the water's edge late in the morning after a journey lasting well over an hour. Claire had packed ham sandwiches with plenty of salad and, true to form, Philip had devoured more than his share on the way. They all had their swimsuits on underneath their normal clothing so changing on the beach was easily done. Claire had a bikini swimsuit and it was more than evident that Harvey liked what he saw for her figure was all that could be desired. They all ran down the beach onto the sand and thence to the water's edge. Harvey and Philip jumped straight into the rather cool sea but Claire was more reticent and preferred to get wet an inch at a time.

Harvey called, 'Come on Claire, make a dash for it.'

However, Claire had her own way of doing things. There was no plunging in for her. To her surprise Harvey ran back to her, lifted her bodily and started to carry her further out into the sea.

Claire struggled and said, 'I'm not a good swimmer, Harvey. I can only do the breastroke well.'

'Then you'll have to do it because I'm dropping you in where it's very deep,' Harvey teased.

He dropped her into the sea, meanwhile making sure that she did not go under.

'Oh I'm sorry,' he said. 'But I've saved you from drowning. Anyway, we're now better acquainted.'

'Whatever do you mean by that?' she asked.

'I've at last been able to hold you in my arms,' he replied, 'and I must say, you're a beautiful person, Claire, all over.'

'You're a cheeky one,' she replied but she loved every minute of it.

There was more splashing about in the sea, coupled with a little swimming, of which most was done by Philip. Harvey was certainly enjoying himself teaching Claire other swimming strokes – or so he said. A welcome lunch followed by an afternoon of suntanning and more swimming brought their day at the seaside to a very pleasant close.

Claire soon got over her difficulty in settling down with a man whose main purpose in life was sorting out people's minds. He himself tried hard not to air his professional abilities but inevitably some leaked through when he accounted to Claire for other friends' actions. He did, however, let his hair down once about his work, although as far as his patients were concerned, professional etiquette demanded that he disclosed little. On one occasion he demonstrated to Claire the complexities of his work by describing to her the type of problem it was his responsibility perhaps not to solve but at least to advise on.

A particular case had actually recently arisen, so no names were mentioned. An unmarried business man, chairman of a small manufacturing company, was suddenly summoned to his father's home a hundred or so miles away. The father was gravely ill and, in fact, died a few days later.

The man naturally took over the funeral arrangements and to his surprise found two ladies, who were clearly not relatives, weeping over the grave. When the funeral ended he spoke to them and it soon became clear that the elder of the two had been his father's mistress and the younger was her daughter.

'Oh dear,' said Claire. 'What a mix-up. Was the younger one his father's daughter?'

'That was never disclosed to me but I am fairly sure she was not – one could only guess,' Harvey went on. 'But the plot thickens. Our man took the mistress and her daughter to tea at his hotel and, of all things, eventually fell in love with the daughter and wanted her to go and live with him. What's wrong with that, you might think, especially as the man and the daughter were in the same age group? No, the problem was that the mother bitterly opposed this union because there was no mention of marriage, the man wanting to carry on just as his father had done. But worse than that, what about if the man's father were also the daughter's father? You see, when the mother came to me for help, a case like this is so complex that I can advise as a counsellor but that is all.'

Claire had listened intently, trying to keep up with all the complications as they arose.

'Whatever happened in the end?' she asked.

'To be honest, I don't know,' he replied. 'I've only told you this to show just how complicated human relationships can be. You see, there is no true love in this story because neither of the men was willing to make a full commitment.'

'That was most interesting,' said Claire. 'No, I don't think I'd make a good counsellor. I can see how essential it must have been to know the relationship between the man and the daughter. Oh dear. You have my sympathy.'

In a way she did find much of this interesting and marvelled at his ability to understand human reactions, although there were times when she was convinced that he was analysing her. But these were minor quibbles. It was an inescapable fact that in simply knowing him and having his manly support made her much happier and, accordingly, her general health improved.

On this subject he once had said, 'Of course you're feeling better, Claire. Look at the treatment you're having – me.'

It was also a fact that Harvey thoroughly enjoyed listening to Claire's musical accomplishments on the piano and, much to her surprise, he seemed to know more about classical music than most people. This was something else which strengthened the bond between them. Moreover, Philip was not forgotten for as soon as he discovered that Harvey knew lots about chemistry, he became his slave for ever. In fact,

Philip was able to recount his explosive exploits at school with pride again, his punishment by the headmaster then almost entirely forgotten. Harvey even read parts of *Chemical Magic* to please Philip. Claire considered that Harvey was being artful in showing such an interest but Philip decided that he was a wonderful chap, besides being a wizard at chemistry.

Inevitably into Claire's mind came the subject of sex. So far Harvey had been the perfect gentleman. He had not broached the subject at all to her, although surely discussion and advice must occur regularly in his work. She mentioned this to Pearl at one of their few coffee sessions.

'Well,' Pearl said, 'Henry was also a non-starter before we were married but I've certainly got him going now. Perhaps your friend doesn't want to lose you by being too forward – just like Henry? He may be cautious also because he sees so much of the trouble it can cause. Then again, perhaps he doesn't believe in sex before marriage – is he religious at all?'

'No, not to any great extent. He certainly doesn't preach religion to me,' answered Claire. 'Anyway I like it this way because he's clearly interested in me for myself, not what I've got to offer.'

Pearl raised the obvious question, 'Will you two get married then?'

'That's a difficult one,' said Claire. 'At the moment he seems to be such a nice and comforting chap that I feel I'm falling head over heels for him. He doesn't ever mention marriage, however. Yet he seems to be so keen to be with me. We love each other's company.'

'But if he does pop the question, will you say "yes"?'

'I suppose I would, although I'm getting very scared. Once bitten, twice shy, don't you think, Pearl?'

'Yes, I can understand,' replied Pearl comfortingly. 'You'll just have to carry on to see where it all leads. I'm so happy with old Henry, I do wish the same for you, Claire. You've had such a run of bad luck lately. It's time you had a break.'

Then it happened. After a few more evenings together,

Harvey announced that early the following week he needed to travel north to attend a symposium. He did not explain to Claire what it was about because, as he said, she wouldn't have found it interesting anyway. The whole affair was programmed to last for four days.

Having had Claire as a constant companion for several weeks, he seemed to have no relish for going, but as he said, 'I have to go, Claire, it's all to do with my work and it's essential that I keep up to date. Believe me, these affairs cost a fortune, several hundred pounds for the symposium itself and then there are the hotel expenses. I'll miss you very much. Will you miss me?'

'Terribly,' answered Claire.

As soon as he had gone, she felt lonely again and tended to make too much of a fuss over Philip. Harvey would be away for four whole days. Would he really miss her as much as she was missing him? She felt she was his only girlfriend, but would he be true to her? Could this break sever their relationship? As Pearl had said about her recent run of bad luck, was she back to square one? There was no way out. She must settle down and hope all would be well when Harvey came back.

In fact, Claire did not have to wait for his return. The first evening he telephoned from the hotel to tell her about the journey, his hotel room and how he was getting on. However, the next evening it was a different Harvey on the telephone.

His voice was shaking as he pleaded, 'Claire, darling. I can't wait any longer. Will you marry me?'

Claire was so relieved, she had no time to think about what was happening to her.

'Of course I will,' she blurted out.

She felt as though a weight had been lifted off her mind and she couldn't care a damn about anything else. Harvey chattered on about how much he was missing her and how relieved he was now that he had popped the question and been accepted, also how glad he was that he and Philip got on so well together. But he had actually proposed marriage, that was all Claire could think about. She remained in a daze, but managed to make suitable replies.

With the telephone call finally ended, Claire could not wait to tell Philip the news. He was up in his room and she burst in, bubbling over with happiness.

'Philip,' she cried. 'Harvey and I are going to be married.'

'Oh, Mum, I'm ever so glad. He's such a nice bloke. And clever too. Will he live with us?'

The question took her by surprise.

'Of course, or we'll live with him. We will all live together somewhere.'

'Well,' the boy queried, 'if we move, will I always be able to have a room of my own like this one?'

'There you go again,' she replied. 'Thinking of yourself. No arrangements about anything have yet been made. Harvey and I have only just decided by phone.'

The remaining two days of Harvey's enforced absence seemed to be so slow in passing, yet within herself Claire was a delightfully happy woman. Eventually Harvey was back and she met him off the train. They were both so contented as they walked arm in arm through the station and then hailed a taxi.

Once in the taxi, 'Claire, darling,' he said, 'you've made me so happy. Here I was, sorting out other people's troubles, all the time with one of my own – a lonely man indeed. It's goodbye to loneliness, we'll have a happy life together. I'll see to that. We'll be together for the rest of our lives.'

Claire could only reply with 'Oh, darling. You've made me so wonderfully happy too.'

There were many things to sort out. Now that their marriage was a certainty, Claire kept wondering about sex. Harvey had not even mentioned it, as though it did not exist. Should she broach the subject or wait for him to do so? If she herself mentioned it first would he consider her a fast hussy or would he be glad she had broken the ice? After all, they were getting married very soon and she did want to please him. For herself she could wait, it was such a short time anyway.

The next day when they were alone together she timidly

enquired, 'What about . . . ? Well, you know, darling.'

He was teasing her, 'The wedding cake?'

'No, you know what I'm trying to say.'

'Of course I know. What do *you* want to do? Don't forget we will be married very soon.'

'I thought you might want . . .'

'Much as I do . . . why not tell me what you really want.'

'Well, we've both been without it for so long – at least I have,' she replied.

'Me too, most definitely,' he said. 'I must have been waiting all this time for you, Claire. But now you've asked me, I would like to hold on until we are married. You are the loveliest thing on my earth, Claire, and you are certainly worth waiting for. I'm not a deeply religious man but I recall that according to the Bible we cannot be true Christians unless we refrain from sexual relations with anybody other than our married partner, meaning simply that we should get married first. I must admit that this law of God is constantly being broken all around us, my work clearly illustrates this, but I still feel it is right for us to wait. I've had to say this so often to my patients so I ought at least to take my own advice, provided that you agree, of course.'

This certainly settled Claire down. Much as she had missed such pleasures, deep down she knew it was right to wait and was relieved that Harvey had convinced her. They would wait and forever after feel they had done the right thing. She summed it up:

'Harvey, of course I'm happy to wait. You are so right and, as you say, it's not long to wait anyway. Much as I would have liked to seal our relationship, it is the respectable thing to do.' Thank Goodness I've sorted this one out, she thought.

Then there was the question as to where they would live. Claire had a detached house with extensive garden more or less in the country, whereas he rented a flat in town. To them both the way ahead was obvious: give up the town flat and live together in Claire's house. Oh well, thought Claire, that would solve Philip's problem – he won't even have to move out of his upstairs den.

Harvey was adamant that he had no need for Claire's money from her work in the hotel, nevertheless he left that decision to her. Without doubt, she wished to continue. She had a very interesting job with piano thrown in – what more could a girl want? They were also at one in deciding how the marriage would be conducted, a church wedding of course, and they dutifully attended the church to hear their banns called. Claire decided not to be married in white, as she was in her first marriage, she still had her bottom drawer containing what remained of her earlier trousseau. It was not to be a grand affair, certainly not outrageously extravagant, neither of them wanted that, just a small reception in a private room at Claire's hotel would be sufficient. Naturally, the standard wedding problem arose, that of catering for a certain number of guests but with the total number rising inexorably. Accordingly, as the great day drew nearer it seemed that the room would be rather overfull but Harvey predicted that nobody would care, they would all join in, making it a happy day for the bride and groom, especially with the help of a little extra sherry and champagne. Also because Claire was well-known and liked by both management and staff, it would be a happy place anyway.

So the great day came. Most of their guests were at the church and although the vicar was unhappy about too much confetti being thrown about, inevitably there was some. Then the photographs – Harvey was holding her hand tightly as if he had no intention of letting her get away. The other guests draped themselves around in true wedding fashion. It was all over quickly. A fleet of cars then took them all to the hotel.

Harvey seemed to have quite a few friends, mostly medical people and some fellow psychiatrists, one or two with the expected psychiatrist-type beards, or as Claire preferred to put it, 'face fungus'. She often said that she preferred her men clean-shaven so Harvey had considered himself lucky to have at least passed that particular test. Claire met and chatted with all the guests and felt relieved that she seemed to have gained one of the few more conventional men, irrespective of the fact that in reality Harvey was 'one of them'. She herself had, as she put it, more orthodox friends and to this classification Harvey readily agreed.

'Generally we are a queer bunch,' he once said, 'at least that's what most people think. I'm the one who's different, of course.'

The happy couple finally took their leave when the taxi arrived to whisk them to the airport, thence to Greece for a short honeymoon – short because Pearl had offered to look after Philip but she could manage the task for a few days only. This certainly took a load off Claire's mind and, anyway, she did not want to burden Pearl with her son for too long. It seemed that the Grecian sun had been waiting for the two lovers to arrive – it shone continually for them. The hotel was on the seashore and was first-class. Somehow the management had discovered that these particular guests were newlyweds and so gave them special treatment. Far from feeling shy when other guests congratulated her, Claire enjoyed every minute of it and especially now that she was known as Mrs Granville. Every day there was swimming in the delightfully warm sea followed by cooling drinks under large sun-shades on the sand. But it was all over so quickly.

So a new chapter in Claire's life began. It had really been worth waiting, for being with Harvey was beyond her wildest dreams. He truly was her soul mate, a man brimming over with love and kindness. She was happier than she had ever been, realizing that marriage to Lionel was nothing compared with what she then had. She had security, help with her son and his future, her own piano and someone very special with whom to share her all. In fact, everything in Claire's garden was lovely and especially the scent of the summer roses.